JUST ONCE

(A Cami Lark Mystery —Book Five)

BLAKE PIERCE

Blake Pierce

Blake Pierce is the USA Today bestselling author of the RILEY PAGE mystery series, which includes seventeen books. Blake Pierce is also the author of the MACKENZIE WHITE mystery series, comprising fourteen books; of the AVERY BLACK mystery series, comprising six books; of the KERI LOCKE mystery series, comprising five books; of the MAKING OF RILEY PAIGE mystery series, comprising six books; of the KATE WISE mystery series, comprising seven books; of the CHLOE FINE psychological suspense mystery, comprising six books; of the JESSIE HUNT psychological suspense thriller series, comprising twenty-eight books; of the AU PAIR psychological suspense thriller series, comprising three books; of the ZOE PRIME mystery series, comprising six books; of the ADELE SHARP mystery series, comprising sixteen books, of the EUROPEAN VOYAGE cozy mystery series, comprising six books; of the LAURA FROST FBI suspense thriller, comprising eleven books; of the ELLA DARK FBI suspense thriller, comprising fourteen books (and counting); of the A YEAR IN EUROPE cozy mystery series, comprising nine books, of the AVA GOLD mystery series, comprising six books; of the RACHEL GIFT mystery series, comprising ten books (and counting); of the VALERIE LAW mystery series, comprising nine books (and counting); of the PAIGE KING mystery series, comprising eight books (and counting); of the MAY MOORE mystery series, comprising eleven books; of the CORA SHIELDS mystery series, comprising eight books (and counting); of the NICKY LYONS mystery series, comprising eight books (and counting), of the CAMI LARK mystery series, comprising eight books (and counting), of the AMBER YOUNG mystery series, comprising five books (and counting), of the DAISY FORTUNE mystery series, comprising five books (and counting), of the FIONA RED mystery series, comprising five books (and counting), and of the new FAITH BOLD mystery series, comprising five books (and counting).

An avid reader and lifelong fan of the mystery and thriller genres, Blake loves to hear from you, so please feel free to visit www.blakepierceauthor.com to learn more and stay in touch.

BOOKS BY BLAKE PIERCE

FAITH BOLD MYSTERY SERIES
SO LONG (Book #1)
SO COLD (Book #2)
SO SCARED (Book #3)
SO NORMAL (Book #4)
SO FAR GONE (Book #5)

FIONA RED MYSTERY SERIES
LET HER GO (Book #1)
LET HER BE (Book #2)
LET HER HOPE (Book #3)
LET HER WISH (Book #4)
LET HER LIVE (Book #5)

DAISY FORTUNE MYSTERY SERIES
NEED YOU (Book #1)
CLAIM YOU (Book #2)
CRAVE YOU (Book #3)
CHOOSE YOU (Book #4)
CHASE YOU (Book #5)

AMBER YOUNG MYSTERY SERIES
ABSENT PITY (Book #1)
ABSENT REMORSE (Book #2)
ABSENT FEELING (Book #3)
ABSENT MERCY (Book #4)
ABSENT REASON (Book #5)

CAMI LARK MYSTERY SERIES
JUST ME (Book #1)
JUST OUTSIDE (Book #2)
JUST RIGHT (Book #3)
JUST FORGET (Book #4)
JUST ONCE (Book #5)
JUST HIDE (Book #6)
JUST NOW (Book #7)

JUST HOPE (Book #8)

NICKY LYONS MYSTERY SERIES
ALL MINE (Book #1)
ALL HIS (Book #2)
ALL HE SEES (Book #3)
ALL ALONE (Book #4)
ALL FOR ONE (Book #5)
ALL HE TAKES (Book #6)
ALL FOR ME (Book #7)
ALL IN (Book #8)

CORA SHIELDS MYSTERY SERIES
UNDONE (Book #1)
UNWANTED (Book #2)
UNHINGED (Book #3)
UNSAID (Book #4)
UNGLUED (Book #5)
UNSTABLE (Book #6)
UNKNOWN (Book #7)
UNAWARE (Book #8)

MAY MOORE SUSPENSE THRILLER
NEVER RUN (Book #1)
NEVER TELL (Book #2)
NEVER LIVE (Book #3)
NEVER HIDE (Book #4)
NEVER FORGIVE (Book #5)
NEVER AGAIN (Book #6)
NEVER LOOK BACK (Book #7)
NEVER FORGET (Book #8)
NEVER LET GO (Book #9)
NEVER PRETEND (Book #10)
NEVER HESITATE (Book #11)

PAIGE KING MYSTERY SERIES
THE GIRL HE PINED (Book #1)
THE GIRL HE CHOSE (Book #2)
THE GIRL HE TOOK (Book #3)
THE GIRL HE WISHED (Book #4)
THE GIRL HE CROWNED (Book #5)

THE GIRL HE WATCHED (Book #6)
THE GIRL HE WANTED (Book #7)
THE GIRL HE CLAIMED (Book #8)

VALERIE LAW MYSTERY SERIES
NO MERCY (Book #1)
NO PITY (Book #2)
NO FEAR (Book #3)
NO SLEEP (Book #4)
NO QUARTER (Book #5)
NO CHANCE (Book #6)
NO REFUGE (Book #7)
NO GRACE (Book #8)
NO ESCAPE (Book #9)

RACHEL GIFT MYSTERY SERIES
HER LAST WISH (Book #1)
HER LAST CHANCE (Book #2)
HER LAST HOPE (Book #3)
HER LAST FEAR (Book #4)
HER LAST CHOICE (Book #5)
HER LAST BREATH (Book #6)
HER LAST MISTAKE (Book #7)
HER LAST DESIRE (Book #8)
HER LAST REGRET (Book #9)
HER LAST HOUR (Book #10)

AVA GOLD MYSTERY SERIES
CITY OF PREY (Book #1)
CITY OF FEAR (Book #2)
CITY OF BONES (Book #3)
CITY OF GHOSTS (Book #4)
CITY OF DEATH (Book #5)
CITY OF VICE (Book #6)

A YEAR IN EUROPE
A MURDER IN PARIS (Book #1)
DEATH IN FLORENCE (Book #2)
VENGEANCE IN VIENNA (Book #3)
A FATALITY IN SPAIN (Book #4)

ELLA DARK FBI SUSPENSE THRILLER
GIRL, ALONE (Book #1)
GIRL, TAKEN (Book #2)
GIRL, HUNTED (Book #3)
GIRL, SILENCED (Book #4)
GIRL, VANISHED (Book 5)
GIRL ERASED (Book #6)
GIRL, FORSAKEN (Book #7)
GIRL, TRAPPED (Book #8)
GIRL, EXPENDABLE (Book #9)
GIRL, ESCAPED (Book #10)
GIRL, HIS (Book #11)
GIRL, LURED (Book #12)
GIRL, MISSING (Book #13)
GIRL, UNKNOWN (Book #14)

LAURA FROST FBI SUSPENSE THRILLER
ALREADY GONE (Book #1)
ALREADY SEEN (Book #2)
ALREADY TRAPPED (Book #3)
ALREADY MISSING (Book #4)
ALREADY DEAD (Book #5)
ALREADY TAKEN (Book #6)
ALREADY CHOSEN (Book #7)
ALREADY LOST (Book #8)
ALREADY HIS (Book #9)
ALREADY LURED (Book #10)
ALREADY COLD (Book #11)

EUROPEAN VOYAGE COZY MYSTERY SERIES
MURDER (AND BAKLAVA) (Book #1)
DEATH (AND APPLE STRUDEL) (Book #2)
CRIME (AND LAGER) (Book #3)
MISFORTUNE (AND GOUDA) (Book #4)
CALAMITY (AND A DANISH) (Book #5)
MAYHEM (AND HERRING) (Book #6)

ADELE SHARP MYSTERY SERIES
LEFT TO DIE (Book #1)
LEFT TO RUN (Book #2)
LEFT TO HIDE (Book #3)

LEFT TO KILL (Book #4)
LEFT TO MURDER (Book #5)
LEFT TO ENVY (Book #6)
LEFT TO LAPSE (Book #7)
LEFT TO VANISH (Book #8)
LEFT TO HUNT (Book #9)
LEFT TO FEAR (Book #10)
LEFT TO PREY (Book #11)
LEFT TO LURE (Book #12)
LEFT TO CRAVE (Book #13)
LEFT TO LOATHE (Book #14)
LEFT TO HARM (Book #15)
LEFT TO RUIN (Book #16)

THE AU PAIR SERIES
ALMOST GONE (Book#1)
ALMOST LOST (Book #2)
ALMOST DEAD (Book #3)

ZOE PRIME MYSTERY SERIES
FACE OF DEATH (Book#1)
FACE OF MURDER (Book #2)
FACE OF FEAR (Book #3)
FACE OF MADNESS (Book #4)
FACE OF FURY (Book #5)
FACE OF DARKNESS (Book #6)

A JESSIE HUNT PSYCHOLOGICAL SUSPENSE SERIES
THE PERFECT WIFE (Book #1)
THE PERFECT BLOCK (Book #2)
THE PERFECT HOUSE (Book #3)
THE PERFECT SMILE (Book #4)
THE PERFECT LIE (Book #5)
THE PERFECT LOOK (Book #6)
THE PERFECT AFFAIR (Book #7)
THE PERFECT ALIBI (Book #8)
THE PERFECT NEIGHBOR (Book #9)
THE PERFECT DISGUISE (Book #10)
THE PERFECT SECRET (Book #11)
THE PERFECT FAÇADE (Book #12)
THE PERFECT IMPRESSION (Book #13)

THE PERFECT DECEIT (Book #14)
THE PERFECT MISTRESS (Book #15)
THE PERFECT IMAGE (Book #16)
THE PERFECT VEIL (Book #17)
THE PERFECT INDISCRETION (Book #18)
THE PERFECT RUMOR (Book #19)
THE PERFECT COUPLE (Book #20)
THE PERFECT MURDER (Book #21)
THE PERFECT HUSBAND (Book #22)
THE PERFECT SCANDAL (Book #23)
THE PERFECT MASK (Book #24)
THE PERFECT RUSE (Book #25)
THE PERFECT VENEER (Book #26)
THE PERFECT PEOPLE (Book #27)
THE PERFECT WITNESS (Book #28)

CHLOE FINE PSYCHOLOGICAL SUSPENSE SERIES
NEXT DOOR (Book #1)
A NEIGHBOR'S LIE (Book #2)
CUL DE SAC (Book #3)
SILENT NEIGHBOR (Book #4)
HOMECOMING (Book #5)
TINTED WINDOWS (Book #6)

KATE WISE MYSTERY SERIES
IF SHE KNEW (Book #1)
IF SHE SAW (Book #2)
IF SHE RAN (Book #3)
IF SHE HID (Book #4)
IF SHE FLED (Book #5)
IF SHE FEARED (Book #6)
IF SHE HEARD (Book #7)

THE MAKING OF RILEY PAIGE SERIES
WATCHING (Book #1)
WAITING (Book #2)
LURING (Book #3)
TAKING (Book #4)
STALKING (Book #5)
KILLING (Book #6)

RILEY PAIGE MYSTERY SERIES
ONCE GONE (Book #1)
ONCE TAKEN (Book #2)
ONCE CRAVED (Book #3)
ONCE LURED (Book #4)
ONCE HUNTED (Book #5)
ONCE PINED (Book #6)
ONCE FORSAKEN (Book #7)
ONCE COLD (Book #8)
ONCE STALKED (Book #9)
ONCE LOST (Book #10)
ONCE BURIED (Book #11)
ONCE BOUND (Book #12)
ONCE TRAPPED (Book #13)
ONCE DORMANT (Book #14)
ONCE SHUNNED (Book #15)
ONCE MISSED (Book #16)
ONCE CHOSEN (Book #17)

MACKENZIE WHITE MYSTERY SERIES
BEFORE HE KILLS (Book #1)
BEFORE HE SEES (Book #2)
BEFORE HE COVETS (Book #3)
BEFORE HE TAKES (Book #4)
BEFORE HE NEEDS (Book #5)
BEFORE HE FEELS (Book #6)
BEFORE HE SINS (Book #7)
BEFORE HE HUNTS (Book #8)
BEFORE HE PREYS (Book #9)
BEFORE HE LONGS (Book #10)
BEFORE HE LAPSES (Book #11)
BEFORE HE ENVIES (Book #12)
BEFORE HE STALKS (Book #13)
BEFORE HE HARMS (Book #14)

AVERY BLACK MYSTERY SERIES
CAUSE TO KILL (Book #1)
CAUSE TO RUN (Book #2)
CAUSE TO HIDE (Book #3)
CAUSE TO FEAR (Book #4)
CAUSE TO SAVE (Book #5)

CAUSE TO DREAD (Book #6)

KERI LOCKE MYSTERY SERIES
A TRACE OF DEATH (Book #1)
A TRACE OF MURDER (Book #2)
A TRACE OF VICE (Book #3)
A TRACE OF CRIME (Book #4)
A TRACE OF HOPE (Book #5)

PROLOGUE

"When your legs get tired, run with your heart," Davina Bright muttered to herself, staring ahead at the unforgiving lights and the endless curve of the indoor track. It didn't look inviting, she thought wearily. Instead, it looked intimidating, and even threatening.

Scraping back a lock of sweaty blonde hair, she forced her aching legs to move, heading out for yet another lap.

The upcoming race, in three weeks' time, was her last chance to qualify for the Boston Marathon next year. Seeing it was in her home city, running this marathon had always been a dream of hers. It was one of the top marathons in the world, and one that thousands of elite runners aspired to.

But numbers were strictly limited, and that meant qualification was tough. This was her third year of trying. She was hoping that in three weeks, she might be able to finish the upcoming qualifier inside the time.

This week was her last of intense training. After this, it would taper off in preparation for race day.

She glanced down, checking her fitness watch, looking at her heart rate and her running time.

"Too slow," she muttered, feeling disappointed with herself, and wondering how it was possible to force her body to give any more speed. Her legs were done! Her feet, in their expensive neon pink running shoes, were aching. Telling herself to run with her heart was no longer helping. That uplifting motivation only went so far.

The fact was, she was exhausted. She'd run for an hour already. She'd finished some intervals, done a few sprints, and now she was on the track going for sheer, torturous distance. She'd gotten here late, and the track manager had agreed for the indoor stadium to stay open another half an hour so she could finish her full workout time. But what use was it if she still didn't qualify? Her legs were killing her, her arms were heavy and weak, and her chest was tight.

She was tired, and also frustrated. Why was it that, after doing so much work, she was still not seeing the results she wanted?

Before she knew it, as she ran, she was cursing under her breath, quietly, angrily, muttering about how she was tired of not making it. This race she was preparing for was her last chance, and she was tired of being tired.

And now, there was someone else in the stadium behind her. What was that all about? She thought she was the last person in here tonight. Now it seemed to be open season.

Whoever else was here, was running fast. A lot faster than she was.

Gritting her teeth, Davina glanced around. Being lapped, right now, was the last thing she wanted. Talk about a humiliating end to a bad session.

The man behind her was running at speed. That was for sure. He was powering along the track, from the far end, all the way toward where she was now. It was as if he was training for a sprint.

And there was something weirdly featureless about his face.

Looking around again, Davina saw, with a jolt, that he was wearing a flesh colored ski mask. It made his entire face look blank. It was as if a faceless man was on this track.

That was her first thought. Her second thought was - why would anyone need to wear a ski mask when training? It wasn't cold, and the track was under cover.

There was something about the intent with which he was running that was scaring her.

Davina was starting to wonder what would happen when he caught up with her. She suddenly realized how alone she was. Just him and her, in this giant, otherwise empty, indoor stadium. Nobody would be here until after she left. She guessed they'd lock up for the night at some stage, but it wasn't as if anyone was waiting for her to leave.

Maybe he had opportunistically come in, and was just planning on doing a quick run. But that mask? It was eerie. Thud-thud-thud, the footsteps approached behind her.

There was a way she could check if he was really just doing some exercise. To her relief, she saw a small track, looping back to the entrance at the halfway mark. This would allow her to get off the main track, and that would mean he would just run past her, and she would stop feeling this vague but intense sense of threat. At least it would set her mind at rest.

The small track was only a few yards ahead. Reaching it, she veered left, now running directly back toward the entrance door. She wiped sweat away from her forehead, aware it was stinging her eyes, but more importantly, it was blurring her vision.

She wanted to see if he was coming after her.

"I'm sure he won't," she mouthed the words, too tired and breathless to speak them aloud. She was probably just exaggerating this entire scenario in her own mind because she was looking for an excuse to quit for the day. Lazy, lazy.

But also scared, in some instinctive way that told her this was bad news, that this man was not just here for exercise.

And as the footsteps veered in her direction, she realized with a shock of fear that she'd been right. He was chasing her. Why else would he veer this way after her? She glanced behind her again. Yes, he was on the smaller track, and he was sprinting toward her with a clear, silent intent in his body language. She was not misinterpreting this. He was chasing her!

"No!" she screamed. "Help!"

But she realized that using her voice was just going to waste energy. Energy she needed to get out of here, to get away from him.

With a new surge of speed, drawing from depths she didn't know she had, Davina sped up. She could do it. She could reach the door ahead of this man, and get out, and get away.

She flung herself forward, nearly losing her balance as her ankle twisted under her, but managing to right herself and speed on, because everything depended on this. The exit door was only twenty yards in front of her now. This was the end of the lap, and she could just run outside, and she would be safe.

It was so close. She was going to make it, she was going to be able to get outside. She grabbed the door, pulled hard.

And cried out in horror. The big door should have swung open easily. But it hadn't. It was stuck fast, closed. Desperately, she struggled with it, banging on it, shaking it.

"Let me out! Help! Let me out!"

She swung around, her back to the door, screaming.

The man with the mask was now racing directly toward her, something gleaming in his hand.

And she was trapped.

CHAPTER ONE

"Ethan, please be okay. Hang in there. It's not as bad as it looks," Cami Lark gabbled, feeling sick with anxiety, her heart constricting. FBI agent Ethan Myers was lying face up on the paving, gasping for breath, his handsome features sheet-white, his lips blue.

Crouched by the side of the road, half shielded by a row of parked cars, she was trying her best to stop the bleeding in his chest wound with her bunched up jacket, but already her fingers were soaked in blood. She shook her black-dyed, edgily shaven hair out of the way, staring down in horror. This had all gone so terribly wrong.

She had asked Ethan to come with her on her personal mission to get a voice recording, so that she could access the laptop she'd stolen from disgraced ex-FBI agent Liam Treverton. Liam was the person who had mishandled her sister Jenna's missing person case, six years ago. Cami suspected he'd been involved with Jenna in other ways, that there was more to their relationship, and to her disappearance.

She'd hacked her way into Liam's house and taken his laptop, but it was proving impossible to open without two factor authentication. She'd found out that he spent Friday nights at this bar, and had asked Ethan to come with her so that she could get a voice recording.

But Ethan had recognized Liam. She didn't know if it was from work, or if they had some other history. He'd hustled her out of the bar. And then, a minute later, as they'd been rushing back to the car, a shooter had opened fire.

Cami had ducked for cover behind one of the cars, and had managed to get Ethan out of the road. But this hiding place was flimsy at best, and she didn't think the shooter had given up yet. She felt consumed by a terror more visceral than any she'd felt before. She feared for Ethan's life, and she feared for her own.

This was the first time, ever, that she'd been targeted in this way.

"Cami, I think I'm going to pass out." Ethan groaned.

"No! Don't pass out. Stay with me, Ethan, we're going to get out of this!"

She had a strong feeling that the shooter had been sent by Liam. It couldn't be a coincidence that someone had shot Ethan in the back, so soon after the men had recognized each other.

Cami didn't think Liam had recognized her. She'd been behind him, so he couldn't have seen her at all. But she was sure that this gunman had meant to get to both of them.

"I've called the ambulance. They should be here any moment," she reassured Ethan, dropping her voice to a murmur because she was now aware the shooter might be listening out for her.

Where was the damned ambulance, and why was it taking so long?

More importantly, where was this gunman? Glancing up, she thought she saw someone sneaking in their direction, looking furtive and purposeful. Was that him, that dark shadow, moving quickly from car to car?

Yes. For a moment, he passed the pool of light from a street lamp, and peering between the cars, Cami glimpsed a better view. It was him, without a doubt, and she saw the shape of the gun, held low by his side.

Cami bit her lip. This was turning deadly. If this man found her and shot her, then without a doubt, they'd both die. She had nothing to fight him with. Ethan had gone with her after working hours and wasn't carrying a gun. Not that Cami knew how to shoot one anyway. A gun wouldn't help her. And all she had in her pocket was her phone, the same phone she'd used to call the ambulance two minutes ago.

If all she had was her phone, she'd better use it, Cami thought, feeling a flash of panic, because if she didn't do something, she knew that this guy was going to be able to get close enough to shoot.

She could see him clearly. There he was. She spotted him running past yet another car, looking from side to side, trying to figure out where they were hiding. This gunman was coming. He was hunting her.

If she told Ethan that he was here, then he would tell her to run, and leave him behind. That she was sure of, but she wasn't prepared to do it, because if she did then Ethan would die. She was trying her best to stop the bleeding, but Ethan, now, was beyond the ability to help her. His hand was cold, and felt limp.

But she had to warn him not to talk, in a way that didn't clue him in that this man was already nearing them.

"We need to keep quiet," she whispered to him. "In case he comes here."

Ethan nodded, wide eyed. She didn't know if he could speak anymore. He was struggling to breathe. His face was cool, with perspiration sheened over it. He didn't look like someone who would survive this, Cami thought, with a stab of utter terror at this thought.

And now, she might not be able to help him.

What could she do to stop this man? She needed to do something, but screaming or shouting for help would only alert him as to where they were. She didn't think he knew yet. For now, he was hunting for them. But if he came much closer then he would find them. And then, for her, it would be over.

Cami wiped her bloodied hand on her jeans. She pulled out her phone, nerves surging inside her, because she already felt like she was all out of options. Could she connect with anything close by? Somehow, she needed to sound the alarm.

Sound the alarm. An idea occurred to Cami. She didn't know if it would work, or how long she would have. But if she could somehow delay him, distract him, get others to the scene, then he might run.

Activating her phone, Cami did a search to see what smart devices she could pick up nearby. There was a smart network in the nearby apartment block, but she wouldn't get into it in time, and couldn't see how it would help anyway. There were a few smart cars. What could she do? Could she log into any of the cars' systems?

Cami activated a program to check, and tried to keep as quiet as possible. She turned back to Ethan, now feeling suffocated with anxiety as she saw he was looking worse.

She checked her phone again.

She'd gotten into the basic controls for two cars in the row. Cami decided she'd better maximize her chances. With shaking hands, she navigated to the alarm activation. Yes. It was available in both cars. This would help her.

Pressing the button, hearing the shriek of the siren, she then turned immediately to the other car, and stabbed that one as well. Now, multiple car alarms were ringing. He'd know that there was going to be some attention here soon. Perhaps he'd run for it.

At any rate, he was clearly hesitating, waiting, and thinking. He wasn't moving forward, like he had been. Every second she could delay him would help. He was listening to those alarms and wondering why his progress was creating this commotion, if there was a thief at work nearby, and whether anyone would be alerted by the noise.

It was enough time. It had bought her what she needed.

Finally, she heard the sound that she'd been waiting for, hoping for. Over the clamor of the nearby alarms, she heard the ambulance, racing in their direction.

"It's here," she whispered to Ethan. "It's all going to be okay, you watch."

But she didn't know if Ethan could hear her. He gave no sign that he'd heard her, and Cami realized, traumatized, that he'd already passed out.

"Please Ethan, be okay!"

She glanced up again to see that the gunman had disappeared. That lurking shadow was gone. As headlights swerved into the street, Cami took a gamble that she'd be safe now. She leaped out from the cars, waving to the ambulance, directing it in, knowing that every moment now counted. The ambulance screeched to a halt, and two paramedics rushed over. Looking at their faces as they examined him, she saw their expressions were grim and serious.

"Do you know what happened?" one of them asked her.

"We were walking down the street. I don't know who it was or why, but someone shot at us and they hit him."

"What about you? Are you okay? Not hurt?"

"I'm fine. But will he be? Do you think he'll pull through?" Tears flooded her eyes.

The medics were already loading him in the ambulance.

"We'll rush him to the ICU. Let's hope he'll be okay."

Even the medic didn't sound too optimistic, Cami realized. This was not just serious but critical.

She had no idea why this had happened. But what she did know was that her own actions had caused this. She'd asked Ethan to come with her on this mission and then things had suddenly unraveled. He'd agreed because there was a spark between them, and they were starting to date.

He'd thought it would be an adventure, and now his life hung in the balance. She felt the harsh weight of guilt, pressing down on her shoulders.

As the ambulance pulled away, speeding to the hospital, Cami felt sick with despair. She'd done what she could to get him help, but now, she had no idea whether Ethan, the man who'd captured her heart, would live or die.

CHAPTER TWO

Cami had been in FBI Agent Connor's office several times in the past. The first time, she'd been pulled in as a criminal who'd hacked the FBI's website. She'd agreed to help with cases that needed IT expertise, in exchange for the FBI dropping the hacking charges against her that would have ended up in a criminal conviction and a long jail sentence.

The next few occasions she'd sat there, it had been preparing for cases, as part of her deal with the FBI.

But this was the first time she'd been sitting here for a debriefing after a crime committed against an FBI agent, even though it was after hours and off duty.

She was seated in between Special Agent Connor, and his boss who headed up the FBI Boston office, Special Agent Fraser. Ethan's shooting was being taken all the way. They wanted answers, and the truth.

It chilled her to look at how serious Connor's face was. And Cami wasn't looking forward to giving answers. It would be traumatic for her to relive this again. It had happened the day before yesterday. Now, it was Sunday morning. Ethan was still in the hospital, on life support, condition critical. And Connor was interrogating her.

"Why were you there?" Connor's strong, heavy-jawed face looked harsher than usual. For once, his brown hair, with threads of gray, looked mussed, as if he'd run his fingers anxiously through it.

Cami agonized over how to answer this. Because it was complicated. Very, very complicated.

Telling Connor the truth would land her in serious trouble. If she admitted that she'd been tracking Liam Treverton, the ex-FBI agent who had botched her sister Jenna's missing person case six years ago, there was a strong chance Connor would contact Liam.

And if he contacted Liam, then Liam might tell him that a week ago, he'd had a strange break-in where someone hacked his smart front door, got inside his house, and stole his laptop.

Connor would put two and two together. Without a doubt, he'd do that. What happened next would go very badly for Cami. It would land her in huge trouble with Connor and his boss, Fraser. And it might also allow Liam to learn who she was. If he heard the name Cami Lark he would instantly connect it with Jenna Lark.

Ethan's reaction when he'd seen Liam had convinced her that this man was dangerous. So then, not only would Cami be in trouble, but she'd also be in serious danger, because Liam would be looking to stop her, and maybe also for payback. Especially when he realized that she was Jenna's sister.

The shooter hadn't been Liam himself, that, Cami was sure of. But the timing was way too much of a coincidence. The gunman had to be connected with Liam. Liam had seen Ethan at the bar, and sent someone after him. That was how Cami interpreted the horrors of Friday night.

"We were in a bar," Cami admitted, in a halting voice.

"The bar down the road from the crime scene?"

"Yes, that one."

"That's not a good place. Ethan knows that. We've had issues there before. Bad things happening."

"We had been walking nearby. We were in the moment," Cami said haltingly. "And then, when we were inside, Ethan grabbed me and said we should go. I don't know why. Maybe he realized where we were, or he saw someone?"

She thought it was best to keep it vague, even though not telling the truth was twisting a tight knot of guilt inside her. She felt wretched about it, but had no choice. That was, basically, what had happened, if you left out her part in it.

"Did Ethan tell you that?" Fraser asked.

Cami shook her head.

"You didn't see who it was?" Fraser pressured her, clearly wanting more detail.

Cami shook her head. "I wasn't aware of anyone threatening him. I was just taking in the ambiance, and wondering if it was a good idea to have a drink there."

Connor frowned, and shrinking inside, Cami realized he didn't believe her.

"Cami, I have to tell you," he said, his tone weary, "I'm starting to wonder if you're trying to hide something."

Cami felt like she'd been slapped. "Do you really think I'm hiding something?"

"This does not sound convincing," he barked. "There must have been a reason for you going there. I know the both of you. You don't randomly stroll into dives like that. Why were you there?"

His voice lashed her. She cringed at the accusation in his tone.

"It was a spur of the moment thing. It was my idea to go there. I suggested it when I saw the place."

"A spur of the moment thing. To go to a bar that has a history of problems?"

"We didn't notice. Or maybe Ethan did, but he thought it would be okay there." She was not letting him crack her. Not this time. She knew how Connor could be, and she was going to stick to her story.

"You didn't notice?" Connor's voice dripped with disbelief. "Please, Cami, you're not that innocent and nor is Ethan. Both of you are street smart. Why are you doing this?"

"If you don't believe it's the truth, there's nothing I can do," Cami lashed back. "Did you never go to dodgy bars when you were younger?"

"Not while working for the FBI, no. I don't believe your version." Connor's voice was stern. "And I need you to tell me the truth. It's not a request. It's an order."

Cami felt breathless. "I don't know what else I can tell you." The knot of tension inside her was growing tighter.

"You can tell the truth!" Connor's voice was rising with each word.

"It's not my fault if you don't believe me!"

"Cami, this isn't the way it's supposed to go."

"How is it supposed to go? I don't know what you expect. We were just having a drink and a night out. There was nothing more to it. We left, we decided not to get a drink; I think he saw someone that worried him there. We were on the street and then he got shot."

"Why were you there?" His voice lashed her.

"Why does it matter?"

"It matters because you went there for a reason that you're hiding from me."

"I don't know what you mean." Cami felt her heart pounding. She was trying her best to keep control, but she felt herself cracking.

"You say Ethan was targeted?"

"I don't know! I don't know, okay? I don't know why he got shot. I don't know what this is about." She didn't want to cry in front of them, but tears were streaming from her eyes again. She'd let everyone down.

10

This was turning into such a disaster, and the man she'd had a love connection with was now fighting for his life.

She knew she was at a total disadvantage here. They were seeing her at the lowest possible point. She was battered, beaten, and feeling broken by what had played out. She didn't know how much longer she could keep summoning enough strength of character to resist this pressure, even though she was going to try and do it for as long as it took.

But every time she thought about Ethan in the hospital, emotion filled her and she felt her resolve crumble.

Connor and Fraser exchanged glances. It was obvious they didn't believe her.

But then, Fraser cleared his throat.

"Leave it be for now," he advised Connor, and Cami stared at him, surprised. Connor glowered, looking frustrated, but Fraser wasn't budging on his stance.

"If it was relevant to anything, I think we'll be able to link it. If it was a private issue, then Cami might not know. And if it was a coincidence, there's nothing more to be learned."

Connor sighed. "I'll leave it then. But I think there's more to it," he said doggedly.

Fraser continued, "Let's go talk about this new case now. We need to find someone to partner with you, to replace her. I'll see you in my office just now. Let me get the case file organized."

"We need to be quick, because the crime scene's still open," Connor agreed.

"Ten minutes," Fraser promised. "Then you can go there."

He stood up and left the room, and Cami stared at Connor feeling shocked.

"Wait a minute. There's a case?" Only now was her brain catching up with the words Fraser had spoken.

Connor nodded, looking frustrated by the entire situation. "It was called in just after you arrived for debriefing. So, while we hunt around to find someone to replace you on it, we're done with you. You can go."

"But - but you mean it involves IT?"

"Yes, it looks like it does."

"And you're not using me?" She stared at him, feeling perplexed and angry.

"How can we use you?" Connor snapped. "We might be demanding but we're not inhumane. You're in no position to handle a case. Look at you." He shook his head.

"I can get myself together! I just need a few minutes."

Cami sniffed hard and scrubbed her eyes. She felt as if she was getting destroyed by what was playing out here. Now, she wasn't even going to be able to help on a case. It wasn't like she was being punished, but the effect was the same. Right now, the only thing she could think of that could possibly atone for what she'd done, would be to jump in and get involved in a new case.

But Connor was shaking his head.

"Cami, no. Now's not the time, and I don't have time to argue with you about this. Go home. I'll update you on it when it's solved." He got up and strode out of the office.

Cami shook her head stubbornly. This was one time she was not going to take no for an answer. She was going to fight to be included, to help catch another killer.

And this time, she was going to win.

"I'm not going home," she muttered, still feeling tearful, but now with a renewed sense of purpose. "If there's one thing I can do to make up for what's happened, it's helping on the case. So, ready or not, here I come."

CHAPTER THREE

Cami knew exactly where Connor parked the unmarked vehicle that he used for work. He parked in the basement, third row from the front, and the remote control that activated the exit boom was always kept in the cubbyhole. He'd press it without even looking.

She knew his habits well, and she was going to try and strategize around them.

Cami felt a weird sense of relief as she headed down to the basemen, because, at last, she was actually doing something. She was taking positive action. This would allow her to make up for the disaster of Friday night.

In fact, she told herself, if she was able to help solve this case, it would surely mean that Ethan would get better? It was like making a deal with life. That's what she was doing now. This was a contract, and she was going to honor her side of the bargain. Somehow, she had to get Connor to accept her help.

That would not be as easy as it sounded, because Connor had made up his mind. He was usually difficult to dissuade from a decision without logical argument, and right now, Cami was not in the mindset for logical argument.

But she was in the mindset for illogical stubbornness, and she had some ideas to get her into a position where she could apply it.

Being star student in her final year at MIT did give her some advantages in that regard, Cami knew. She had access to the dark web, and she was friends with an entire network of some of the best hackers in the world. She had been taught many skills by people who believed the world was a better place if the bad guys were defeated. By 'the bad guys,' different definitions could apply, according to who was talking at the time.

A minute later, she was down at the basement level, approaching Connor's car.

It was locked. And it wasn't a smart car. Connor was somewhat of a technophobe when it came to IT. He was most definitely a people person, and action person, and hands-on person in their partnership.

13

She was the tech geek. He unlocked his car with a normal remote control that would be difficult to hack into.

But there was a gate that opened out of the FBI garage and onto the street. That had more potential, because it was operated from a broader wireless network that she thought she could get into.

Quickly, Cami tested that idea. She knew she wasn't in the best mind frame for concentration right now. But at least she had the best software. Since she'd started working for the FBI, she'd begun seeking out programs that could swiftly crack barriers and defenses. She'd learned how important it was to work fast under pressure, when things needed opening. Or, of course, to stay closed. And now was one of those times.

Okay, it wasn't going to work immediately. After all, this was the FBI and even on basic devices like exit gates, they had a high level of security. But Cami had a higher level of hacking skill. She was exceptionally skilled, in an environment that was hungry for that know-how. That was the only reason she'd gotten a plea deal with the FBI, and hadn't been sent to jail.

So, technology wise, she was ahead of the game, but right now, in these circumstances, time was still a big factor. Fraser had said ten minutes, but in Connor's book, that probably meant five.

Connor was busy, and he hated sitting at his desk. Fraser was even busier and stretched to the limits in his demanding, responsible job. This briefing was going to be ultra short, she felt sure.

She frowned at her phone. Come on, she encouraged it. Do what you need to. Give me this gate's controls.

At that moment, she saw a figure hurrying down the stairs. She grimaced in frustration, because time was up. It looked like Connor. It was his stance, his build.

Damn it, she thought. She was going to be too slow. Connor - now she could see him clearly - was hurrying over to his car, clearly in a rush. He was heading out, going to the crime scene without her. He was going to make it there in time to partner with someone who wasn't her.

Cami clenched her fists and felt a sense of dismay, as if this would mean she'd lost out on her contract with life, as if she'd tried to make a reckless bargain with fate, and had failed.

But then, her phone buzzed.

She glanced down quickly. At last, the program had worked. The access to the gates the FBI used to control vehicle entry was coming up on her phone. And here was the one she needed.

As Connor's car sped toward it, the gate began rattling open.

Hiding behind the nearest parked car, Cami pressed Close on her console, imagining Connor's moment of surprise as the gate reversed direction, and started doing the opposite of what it should.

He was going to try and open it again, and she couldn't let him. Working as fast as she could, Cami activated the gate's locking mechanism as soon as it was fully closed. And then, she got out of the way, ducking behind the nearest parked car to see how this played out.

She could see Connor in the car, impatiently pressing and pressing the button.

"Come on!" he said aloud. But the gate remained locked.

He tried again. And again. She could see he was feeling frustrated and angry. It was obvious in his body language, the way he was stabbing down on that remote, the tightness of his hand on the wheel.

Cami decided it was time to make her move.

She stepped out from behind the car and saw Connor's head immediately turn in her direction.

There was a two-second pause, during which time Cami knew that Connor had figured out exactly what was happening. He buzzed the window down.

"Unlock the gate, Cami," he said, in tones that told her he was all the way at the edge of his temper.

"No," she said. "We still have something to discuss."

"This isn't a time for interfering like this! Stop delaying things," he pressured her.

"Then bring me along," she insisted.

"You're in no state to handle a case now!" Connor argued.

"I think I am."

"And I don't think you are."

"I just hacked your exit gate. You got a problem with my skills right now?"

"I've got a problem with your focus. You're in pieces."

"Well, who are you going to get to work with you? I don't see anyone in the passenger seat, in pieces or not. Maybe I'm missing somebody. Oh, wait. Maybe there isn't anyone!" She glared at him, feeling as mad as he did now.

"There's an agent in another state who's going to be available at the end of day today. He's being flown in tomorrow," Connor said.

It was a clear picture of the current skills gap the FBI was struggling with in tech, and Cami made sure she used it to her advantage.

"Tomorrow?" Cami replied. "You always tell me how important time is on a case. Now you're saying you're going to spend a whole day on your own, without a partner who has good IT skills? That's an unacceptable delay. I can at least help you for now," she pleaded.

Connor sighed. She could see she'd gotten through to him. And also, she thought, he was starting to understand that right now, she needed a job to do and wanted to help.

With a sigh, he relented.

"I'll take you along today. On a trial basis," he warned. "Any problems, any signs that Ethan's situation is taking away from your focus on the case, and it's over. You go home."

Cami felt a sense of deep relief that she could go ahead with her side of the deal.

"Okay," she said. "I can accept that. Thank you for giving me the chance. I won't let you down, Connor. I promise."

She'd gotten her way. And now she was ready to work. She knew if she was going to help Connor, she was going to be working hard Hopefully there would be no time to lose focus.

Connor unlocked the car. Cami heard the locks snap open as she rushed around to the passenger side.

"Okay, then," Connor conceded. "Now open the damned gate."

As she scrambled in, she pressed the button to unlock the gate. Immediately, it slid smoothly back.

Connor hit the gas, and sped out of the garage and onto the road. Fastening her seatbelt, Cami stared firmly ahead.

"Are we on the way to the crime scene?" she asked firmly. Crime scenes were not her favorite place, but she was going to do her best to find this killer, no matter what it took.

Glancing at her, looking surprised by her tone of voice, Connor then reached behind him, grabbed a folder off the back seat, and handed it to Cami.

"Here are the details on the case," he said. "You'd better read it, and get up to speed, as fast as you can, because what this killer is doing is seemingly impossible."

CHAPTER FOUR

"Impossible?" Feeling perturbed, Cami grabbed the folder as Connor continued.

"This crime scene is still active, and it's just ten minutes away. That's where we're going, to see if there's any evidence to be found."

Crime scenes had always been a stumbling block for Cami, but this time she promised herself that whatever horrors this scene held, she was going to deal with them. For Ethan, she was going to do this.

Connor sped down the main road, and veered onto a side road. Cami saw signage for a large sports and athletics complex located a couple of miles ahead. Was this where they were going?

Quickly, she paged through the case file, so that by the time they got there, she would have a better understanding of the case.

Three female athletes had died so far, each one while they had been training alone, Cami read, feeling horrified and intrigued.

"They all seem to have had heart attacks?" she asked Connor, who was waiting impatiently at a red light.

"Yes. They all seem to have heart attacks while training, but there are signs that they were all involved in a struggle prior to death. Marks, bruises on their arms that couldn't be explained from their workout. One had a shoe missing. Another had lost her hair tie. And most puzzling of all, a number was scrawled on their arms in permanent marker. The first victim had the number 195. The second one, I can't remember, and the third, who was called in this morning, had 180."

"So it's like an unknown killer chased them, struggled with them, and then caused them to have a heart attack, before writing a number on their arm?" Cami asked incredulously. She recognized one of the victims' names. Lynne Horwood was a well-known Boston track athlete. She'd been in the Olympics a few years ago, Cami remembered. At any rate, she'd been famous enough for Cami, who didn't take much interest in sports, to have heard of her.

"Scared to death, was the explanation put forward by one of the cops who attended the second scene, which was Jill Whiteley's murder. It stuck," Connor said. "I am sure there's more to it and that's what we need to find out."

"If they'd been outrunning a killer, while training hard, could that have caused a heart attack?"

"I'm not buying that, not three different women."

Cami also didn't buy that three fit, tough-minded athletes could have been run down until they dropped, or else scared to death. Neither explanation sounded likely. But being pursued by a killer who then managed to murder them in an undetectable way seemed like a plausible scenario and it was chilling.

Having been chased by the gunman, the knowledge of what that felt like was fresh in her mind. It was terrifying. Not 'scared to death' level, but 'scared enough to keep running to save your life' level.

"So the killer is chasing these women, and somehow when he's catching them, he's doing something that causes their heart attacks?" Cami was struggling with the concept all over again. All of them? "And there's no sign of anything?"

"No sign so far."

"That's crazy! Surely he must have done something, especially if he got into a struggle with them? Surely there's more to it? Could he have suffocated them during the struggle, or something like that?"

"A possibility," Connor said, signaling and turning into the sports complex. "That's the sort of question we need to think about. I also don't buy 'scared to death' or 'chased to death' and we need to look further. But here we are, so we can see what happened to this recent victim. Her name is Davina Bright."

"Davina Bright," Cami repeated, feeling it was important to know the name, and the personality, that this woman had before her tragic death.

Connor pulled up near the main entrance gate. It was a huge complex, Cami saw. To the right was the large stadium, and to the left, a number of smaller buildings and outdoor training facilities.

Cami saw that two cop cars and an ambulance were parked outside the complex, but as Connor parked, the ambulance pulled slowly away.

They climbed out and headed over to the sports complex entrance.

There, a frantic looking caretaker, in cleaning overalls, and a man in a blue tracksuit that Cami guessed was the manager, were speaking to two policemen.

Cami headed over with Connor to hear what they were saying.

"FBI," Connor introduced himself briefly, showing his badge as the cops nodded a greeting. "What's the background here, please?"

"Davina booked the track arena late last night. After hours. When I checked the door, it was locked," the manager said, sounding agonized, his brown eyes wide in his lean, tanned face. "I thought one of the coaches must have locked up, and that she had left. I never checked inside!"

"Is there another way in?" Connor asked.

"Yes, there's a service entrance, and of course the underground tunnel that leads down into the changing rooms that are used for the big games. But our athletes who train late always use the main entrance that leads into the parking lot."

However, there had been other ways in. This killer could have sneaked in via one of the less direct routes, blocked or locked the main doors, and then pursued this poor woman who had been training on her own. That was creepy, Cami thought with a shiver.

"So you went home last night?"

"Yes, I went home!" He looked aghast that he'd done this. "I checked the doors, saw the lights were off, and then left. I feel so terrible now."

Connor shook his head. "By then, the victim was already deceased. You couldn't have known. And what happened this morning?"

"Our earliest booking was for eleven a.m.," the manager explained. "So Cody went in to do the cleaning at nine, and found her there."

"She was lying by the door," Cody said, shaking his head as if trying to shake away the memory of that moment. "I saw there was a scrape on her arm, and one of her earrings had come loose and was lying beside her. Her watch was also broken. I knew immediately that this was serious, that she must have been attacked. I checked her pulse. I admit I was panicking, but I was trying to remember what to do in such a situation. There was no pulse. I called the cops, and our manager, immediately."

Cami thought that even though the two men had been traumatized and shocked, it seemed they had done everything correctly.

"Is the scene still being checked?" Connor asked.

"Yes, we have forensics there now," the cop said.

"Let's go and take a look," he said to Cami.

As Cami followed him down to the covered track, she found her own mind veering back to Ethan. The sight of him. The sound of his breathing as he struggled for air. The fear as she'd seen the gunman moving from car to car, searching for them.

That nightmare moment had changed their lives, and she felt another rush of anxiety for Ethan. Would he survive? Was it a good or a bad thing that he'd been on life support for more than a day already?

Then, Cami pushed the thought firmly aside, because stressing about Ethan would not help her now. The only thing it would do was ensure Connor kicked her straight off this case if he realized she was getting distracted by this. She couldn't afford distractions and needed to focus.

There, by the main door, she saw crime scene tape had been stretched around an area of a few square yards. Right by the doors was where she'd ended up, and Cami recoiled from the fear she must have felt.

They stopped well before the scene, and put on gloves, head covers, and foot covers. Cami hoped that if there had been a struggle, there might be some trace evidence left by the killer. But since there had been none at the other two scenes, she was worried he might have been too sneaky.

There was the earring, marked by a number that the police had placed there.

And there was the watch. It, too, was lying on the artificial turf with a number placed beside it.

Looking closely at it, Cami saw it was a fitness watch, that this athlete had clearly been using to train.

Fitness watches, like most smart devices, were usually hackable.

An idea came to Cami. Perhaps there was more evidence that could be obtained from this scene - the actual physical track of what Davina had been through.

"I'm going to see if I can get into that watch," she muttered.

She had an idea about what that number scrawled on Davina's arm might mean.

Would she be right? It would depend what information that watch had recorded before its owner died in terror.

CHAPTER FIVE

Opening her phone and starting up the program she needed, Cami began trying to access the victim's discarded watch. The strap had broken, but the watch itself looked fine. And it had enough battery life left to last another hour or so. She guessed that the watch had simply hibernated after Davina had died, with no vitals to monitor.

What could she learn from this chilling information?

Her program had gotten hold of the Bluetooth signal. Now, she needed to go back into the stored records.

Here was the start of Davina's workout. This was where she'd set the device to track her run.

"See here," she told Connor. "I've communicated with her watch, and look what it's showing me."

He leaned over, staring down at the screen.

"This is where her workout began," Cami said, pointing to the place. "You can see here, she was doing this very scientifically. She had alarms set for when she needed to speed up and slow down, and also notifications if her heart rate went over, or under, a certain range. So she was taking this session seriously."

"Yes, I can see the parameters," he said.

"Here's the first hour." Quickly, Cami dragged her finger along the screen, speeding past the small fluctuations. "This was a long session. I'd guess it might have been her final training run before an event."

She followed the graphs and stats as the run progressed. Clearly, Davina had been tiring. Her speed had gradually bled away yet her heart rate remained high.

But then, something had happened.

Cami gasped as she saw the speed make a steep upward jump. Davina had accelerated, fleeing along.

"She must have seen him here," she said. "She knew something was wrong, for sure. Look how she started running. Here's her speed."

"And the heart rate, climbing into the red," Connor observed.

Now, Cami was noting something else.

"She must have been by the doors here. Because now the speed is stationary. But her heart rate is still spiking."

"She was fighting with him for sure," Connor said, looking at the evidence that the watch was giving. A woman who was now not moving, but a heart rate that was still stratospheric. She'd been struggling for her life. He'd caught up with the tiring woman - not difficult along an inside track with locked doors - and had attacked her.

Then, abruptly, the heart rate froze.

"That's the moment the watch broke off her wrist," Cami said. "While she was fighting him. I guess after that, she died, but because the watch fell off her wrist, we can't see the moment of death. The struggle was a couple of minutes long, though."

She took a look at the number on the watch's display. And in her mind, she made the connection that she'd wondered about when she'd wanted to check the watch.

It had been right, and she felt as if she'd taken a step into the killer's mind.

"Connor, look! This watch stopped recording her heart when it was at 180 beats per minute. And that's exactly the number that was written on her arm."

"Yes, so it is." Connor sounded intrigued.

"Her watch would have been live at the time, displaying the info. Do you think he saw it and noted it down? Did he want to show that the speed of her heart, before it stopped, was important?"

"That's a definite link with the reading on the fitness device," Connor agreed. "Well done, Cami. This could be important, and we can take it further. It gives us an insight into his mind. Not into his method, though."

There was still no way of knowing exactly what had played out, whether she had been smothered or suffocated in some way by this man, or whether he'd used another way to make her die before recording her heart rate on her arm.

"He must have worn gloves," Connor said. "Maybe a mask, as well. Because there's nothing here. Forensics are not finding anything." He sounded frustrated.

Being pursued by a masked killer, this athlete would have known she was in trouble. Cami could imagine how she must have decided to get out, to get away. She'd rushed for the doors, and she had then found, to her horror, that they were locked.

She felt an intense pity for this woman, for all these victims. Being chased down and hunted felt a lot more personal to Cami after her own ordeal on Friday night.

22

"There's not a lot more to see here," Connor said. "But all the bodies are at the main pathology office here in Boston. The coroner will be busy with the postmortem now. Let's head there and see what he can tell us.

Normally, this was the part of an investigation that Cami had the biggest problem with. Flashbacks to her sister's disappearance became harsh reality when she was confronted by the autopsy tables.

It was a place that brought all her worst fears to life. But this time, Cami found she could handle the thought of it. She would face anything - anything - if it somehow meant that Ethan might survive. If Cami being brave could make him survive, then brave she would be.

"Let's go and see what the pathologist has to say," she said firmly, her tone causing Connor to stare at her once again in surprise.

***

The pathologist's offices were busy at eleven a.m. on a Sunday morning. Cami could see that the chaos of a Saturday night, with its fights and collisions, drunk driving and brawling, was making itself known. The place was a hive of activity. Technicians were rushing along the corridors. Gurneys were being wheeled into autopsy rooms and storage areas.

Under the bright interior lights, with the cold air hissing from the vents and the suffocating smell of disinfectant, it was easy to forget that outside was a sunny fall morning. In here, it was a very different atmosphere.

"We're looking for the autopsy room for Davina Bright," Connor said to the harassed looking attendant at the front desk.

"Room five. Autopsy's just been done, but the doctor's still in there," she said.

Quickly, Cami pulled on a new set of PPE, including a mask. She remembered well how suffocating this mask had felt the very first time she'd worn it. Now, it didn't feel the same way.

Her heart was pounding, but she was able to breathe regularly and didn't feel like she was about to choke, or pass out. This was the challenge she had to face. And she had to do it, for Ethan.

"You're doing fine," Connor muttered in approval as they walked along the corridor.

They tapped on the door, and it was opened almost immediately by a pathologist who was still gowned and masked. Cami's gaze veered immediately to the steel table, where the body was draped in sheets, to her relief.

Behind the head covers, mask, and layers of PPE, Cami saw the pathologist was a short man with a slight build, a lined face, and wise blue eyes.

"FBI Agent Connor," Connor said. "Assisted by IT expert Cami Lark. Doc, we need to get your take on these murders."

The doctor nodded. "I've handled all three autopsies. It's a puzzling situation. All three women were very fit. Extremely healthy. And it's as if their hearts just stopped. Each one had a massive heart attack."

"Cause?" Connor asked.

"I guess the first and most obvious explanation would be that the heart was overworked. Which would have been difficult, given their levels of fitness. I'm getting a toxicology report, but as you know, that will take more than a week, even prioritized."

"Yes, it's a pity about that delay."

Connor moved to the shrouded corpse, causing Cami to tense. But then, she walked there, too. Connor wasn't peeling back the whole sheet. He was just moving it enough to take a look at the victim's fingers and toes.

He looked at the spaces between them, peering down intently, and Cami suddenly remembered that one of the victims had been missing a shoe.

"Are you looking for needle marks?" she asked.

"Yes," he said. "I'm wondering if this killer injected them with something that could have caused this cardiac arrest."

"I looked for needle marks in all three of the victims, and didn't find any. But it does seem likely that it could be a cause. I was thinking of that, and then started wondering again if it could have been suffocation with something soft. But there's no signs of that either," he admitted.

"This killer is clever. He's been smart enough to leave no trace," Connor said. "I'm saying 'he' because it's clearly the work of a fast, strong individual. But that might also mean he chose an undetectable place to inject. He would have been able to do that if he overpowered them."

"Indeed," the pathologist said.

"The heart rate seems important to him. My partner, Cami Lark, noticed that Davina's fitness watch had last recorded a heart rate of 180, which was the number scrawled on her arm."

24

The pathologist's eyebrows shot up. "That's a very good logical connection. It would make sense, because Lynne Horwood had the number 195, and Jill Whiteley had 178. So yes, all very high, all heart rates that could be achieved during an intense struggle."

"Were they all wearing fitness watches?"

"Yes. They all were. Unfortunately, the two watches belonging to the earlier victims are now non operational because the batteries are drained. We'd need to recharge them and open them to check if the heart rate at the time of death matches that number. But the packages are over there."

While Connor and the pathologist returned to discussing possible injection sites, Cami took a look at the numbered packages which represented the items that had been on the victims' persons when they had been found.

They had all been wearing a fitness device, she saw. She guessed that was standard. These were athletes who had been training. Of course they would wear such devices.

The first victim, Lynne Horwood, had been wearing blue athletics shorts, a gray top, her fitness device, and running shoes. The second one, Jill Whiteley ... now this was interesting, Cami thought.

In her pile of possessions, along with the clothing, Cami saw the distinctive shape of a pepper spray cannister. For someone who'd been training at the time, carrying pepper spray might be unusual. Perhaps it pointed the way to a recent threat, or incident.

Had Jill Whiteley escaped the killer once, and taken precautions to make sure she didn't get attacked again? If she'd been living in fear, they needed to find out who, exactly, she'd been so afraid of.

CHAPTER SIX

"Connor, I see that Jill Whiteley was carrying pepper spray with her," Cami said, as soon as Connor was finished speaking to the pathologist. "Look here. It's in the bag with her possessions. It was on her at the time."

"She clearly didn't get the chance to use it," Connor said thoughtfully. "But yes, why did she have it on her at all? She was using the track at a local gym when she died. She wasn't running through urban backstreets. Why the spray?" He paused. "If I'm correct, from the case report, that gym was also where Lynne Horwood worked out occasionally. So there could be a link there."

"Can we find out if she had any trouble with anyone at the gym, or someone who might have followed her there?" Cami asked, feeling another pang of regret, because if Ethan had been in the office, then he would have been able to do this for them in the blink of an eye. "I'm no expert on these things, but I wouldn't have thought she'd be carrying it on her during her training. Perhaps she had it for protection for some other reason?"

"We need to look into that. I think we're done here." He turned to the pathologist. "I'd like you to examine these bodies again. Let's imagine we're dealing with a clever and murderous psychopath, who has planned these kills and knows how to hide any trace of himself. Not in the normal spectrum of cunning. And see if that takes us anywhere."

"Will do," the pathologist promised.

Connor turned and left the mortuary room, with Cami hurrying along behind him, feeling relieved that this part of the investigation was behind her.

As she peeled off her PPE, Cami heard Connor on the phone, talking to someone else in his office.

"We're going to need to look into Jill Whiteley's background in more depth. Any trouble she was involved in, any cases she opened, I'd like you to look it up and let me know."

He disconnected, and turned to Cami. "I see Jill's closest relative here in Boston is her sister, Aimee. Let's go and speak to Aimee and get some information from her."

26

Cami hurried to the car, scrambling in, checking the date of Jill's death once again as Connor sped out into the bright Sunday morning. Jill had died three days ago, and that meant her sister would still be emotionally wrecked. Cami knew this was going to be a difficult conversation.

"I see Aimee lived close to where Jill did. Same suburb," Connor said, glancing at the map, and down at the case file which Cami had open. That was good, Cami knew, because living in the same suburb would increase the likelihood that the sisters were close. Hopefully, Jill had shared any trouble or fears with her sister.

As Connor wound his way through the streets, his phone rang again.

"Hello, Connor speaking?"

There was something about the sharp note of concern in his voice that got Cami's pulse instantly racing.

Was this the hospital, calling with news on Ethan?

She waited for Connor to speak, her stomach clenching, the tension in her rising. Had Ethan died? Or had he improved enough to come off life support?

She felt sick and dizzy at the thought he might be dying.

But Connor wasn't giving anything away. He spoke in monosyllables. A quick "Yes," a brief, "Noted," and then he thanked the caller and cut the call. Cami wanted to ask, but she decided not to.

If this was a different reason for a phone call, it was better that Connor didn't get reminded of how worried she was about Ethan's condition. She was sure he did know, but she'd promised not to let it affect her work on this case.

"This is where Aimee Whiteley lives." Connor said.

They were in a neighborhood full of small, neat houses that seemed to have a family feel. Cami saw a mother and two kids crossing the road, heading for a park with swings and a climbing frame. Two teens were skateboarding on a side street. A man was at work in his garden, clipping a hedge.

Connor pulled up outside a neat little brick house with a red Mini parked in the driveway outside. Cami got out of the car and walked up the path with him.

Connor rang the doorbell, and after a pause, a young woman answered. Remembering the ID photo from the case file, Cami saw she had the same dark hair and eyes as Jill Whiteley. She looked to be in her late twenties and had a stressed expression.

"FBI," Connor said, showing her his badge. "Ma'am, are you Aimee Whiteley?"

"Yes, I am," she said, her voice wobbling. "I guess you want to ask some questions about Jill?"

"If you're able to answer them now." Connor's voice was courteous. "I understand you must be very upset, but the information will help the case."

"Sure. I guess I can. The police did speak to me, the day after it happened. Come in."

She led them through to a small living room. There, Cami felt touched to see that there were several photos of Jill on the coffee table, together with a large candle that was burning.

"I'm so devastated by this. We were very close," she said, collapsing down on the couch, looking at the photos and blinking rapidly.

Cami and Connor seated themselves on the couch opposite.

"I'm so sorry," Cami said.

"Tell me about Jill's life. Was she in a relationship?"

"No. She was single. We're both single. Jill was a triathlete. She was passionate about her sport, and she was hoping that she might be selected for one of the state teams, and be able to take her talent further."

"So she trained very hard for it?" Connor asked sympathetically.

"Yes. She'd been training hard all year. That was her life, really. She'd been doing sports since she was a kid. It was an important part of who she was."

Aimee's eyes were tearful, her face tense with grief. Cami could see how upsetting it was to think of her sister having been murdered. She guessed Aimee was trying really hard to hold back floods of tears.

"Did she have any enemies, people who might have wanted to hurt her?" Connor asked.

"No. No way. She wasn't that kind of person at all. She never fought with anyone. Her day job was at the gym. When she wasn't training herself, she was working with her clients."

"Any difficulties with people at the gym? Anyone making unwelcome approaches to her?" Connor's voice was serious. "We noticed she was carrying pepper spray. Was there a reason for that?"

Now, Aimee narrowed her eyes thoughtfully.

"Pepper spray? That's reminding me of something. She did mention pepper spray. And it wasn't something she usually carried. She always joked that she didn't scare easily," Aimee said.

Cami waited anxiously, hoping she'd remember. And she did. She nodded decisively.

"She told me that there had been some issues at her gym, that a number of the clients had complained that they'd been harassed by some lurker, and that she'd had to take steps against him herself. But it wasn't anyone she knew. It was just some random stranger. Do you think he could be the killer?" she asked, looking horrified anew. "I didn't tell the police. They just asked if anyone had been following her around, or if she had fought with anyone. I didn't think about this man."

"Sometimes, you only remember details at a later stage, but it's important for us to follow up," Connor said. "All the information we can get will be important. Did Jill make an official complaint against him?"

"She said she was going to, but I didn't hear any more about it. Unfortunately, I was sick with the flu last week, and so we didn't get together like we usually did. She avoided people with the flu, because being so fit made it risky to catch viruses since she had a race coming up. So I never got to find out."

"You've been very helpful," Connor praised.

And she had. As they stood, offering their sympathies again, Cami knew this had been a very productive visit. First, they had found out that Jill didn't scare easily. If she'd run from a suspected killer, she would have had a very good reason - and Cami doubted she would have been 'scared to death.'

And secondly, she'd laid a complaint against someone who had not only been harassing her, but also other women. And that definitely pointed to the likelihood of serial crimes.

As soon as Connor was out of the house. he got on the phone again to find out more about incidents at the local gym where Jill had trained and worked.

"Is there any record?" he asked whoever he was speaking to. Then he nodded. "Thanks."

He turned to Cami.

"The man who was harassing the gym goers was given a warning by local police, and was removed from the area after complaints, but the police said nobody had yet pressed charges. However, they do know who he is. His name is Dirk Fisher, and he lives just a few blocks from the gym. He apparently works for a pharmaceutical company." Connor's face was thoughtful, and Cami knew he was being reminded of those strange cardiac arrests. "Let's go and speak to Mr. Fisher immediately," he decided.

CHAPTER SEVEN

The killer had a growing collection of masks. From the featureless, blank, and terrifying ski mask he'd used recently, to the ultra-scary Joker mask with its wide, bloody, haphazard grin.

Every time he set out to try to get his revenge, he would wear a different one. Depending on his mood, of course.

Last night he had been feeling blank, with an overdose of rage, feeling that the world was just too much for him. And so he'd chosen the mask with the blank features. He'd enjoyed using it. It had been a good disguise to have worn when meting out his payback.

But it had been worn and thrown away, and now he was adding to his collection again.

He was in a party shop, searching through the stack of Halloween masks, now on sale, as Halloween had recently passed.

"Can I help?" the sales assistant asked. She was a blonde woman, with wide, blue eyes. Immediately, he knew that she wouldn't trigger his anger. She wasn't the type that he'd been compared to all his life. She was curvaceous, with a plump, pretty face. The kind of woman who probably tried to force herself to go for a weekly gym session, and mostly failed. The kind of woman who would eat a good dinner and then not be scared to have dessert afterward.

This was the kind of woman - the kind of person - that he felt comfortable with.

He smiled at her. He knew that when he was in a good mood, he was a good looking guy. She'd find nothing in him to be scared of, when he wasn't wearing a mask.

"I'm looking for a few masks. Got to do some plays, with my nieces and nephews. We're always running short of characters."

"Sounds like fun," she said. "How about Batman?"

That was too distinctive, he thought.

"We've done that," he said regretfully.

"How about a pirate?"

He smiled. "Now you're talking," he said.

She held out the pirate mask. It had a ragged beard, a leather eye patch, a scar on the cheek, and a tilted hat. It was a good mask, apart from one problem. The eye patch covered one of the eye holes, and he needed both his eyes to catch his prey.

However, it wouldn't be a bad thing to buy it anyway. It only backed up his story.

"This is a cute one. A bumble bee. Very unusual."

She held it up. It also wasn't right for him. It was too cheerful. The bumble bee had a smiling face, and it looked kind and non-dangerous. He wanted terror to be the final emotion in his victims' hearts.

He liked to think of himself as a character when he was wearing his masks. He liked to think of himself as someone else. And he knew that the mask he selected would be something that would give him an angle, a logical reason for his actions.

"I need scarier ones than that," he insisted. "My nieces and nephews are horror fans."

"Oh, we have a few of those. They're more expensive, though," she said, smiling.

"I don't care," he said.

She turned and moved away to where a small rack of masks was tucked away. She took one off it, and brought it back to him. It was in the shape of a skull. Wide, empty eye sockets, sharp cheekbones, dark shadows, and grinning teeth. The skull was absolutely perfect. He knew as soon as he saw it, that he wanted to wear it when he was on the hunt.

"Perfect," he praised her.

"Or this one?"

"That's great," he said.

It was a devil's mask, with a red, curling mouth, dark, flashing eyes, and vicious sharp horns. That mask was perfect. He imagined arriving at his next prey wearing this. How terrified she would be. It would be the ultimate send-off, looking into that snarling face.

He took it down from the shelf.

"You're sure you don't want the bumble bee?" she asked, sounding disappointed.

"Not this time. This one is definitely the best, and I'll also take the pirate, and the skull," he said, and handed over his card.

She was looking at him, and he felt something stir. She was pretty. He liked the curve of her lips, and the color of her hair. But he didn't want to be attracted to her. He had to get over this bump in the road, and make sure that he'd vanquished the demons of his past. He could never have a normal life, with a normal woman, while he was damaged goods.

Even so, he knew he liked her.

He liked her better than the other women, who all liked to think they were so much better than he was. Those were the ones that awakened his monsters.

He smiled at her, and she responded with a nervous smile of her own.

"Have a nice day," she said, and she sounded as if she genuinely meant it.

"Oh, I will," he said, and he knew he'd enjoy every moment of it. Perhaps he'd come back and shop at this place again, soon. It was a good experience. The interaction with that woman had been calming. She'd done nothing to antagonize him. Not like the others.

He knew he had to put his mask on as soon as he could. He didn't have time to lose. It was time to hunt again, and he felt the familiar anger rise inside him as he saw the vivid neon signage of the gym across the road.

There were so many of these women, and his job was so frustratingly slow. Doing the research, choosing the right prey, finding out when they would be alone: it all took time. And, of course, his signature, the all important heart rate before the death throes began.

He knew he would end up in jail if he were caught, and that planning properly was essential. Even so, he knew he couldn't wait much longer. He had to do what he'd set out to do, and he had to do it soon.

"I'm ready for you," he said.

He could feel his body starting to burn with his anger, and he knew he had to stop off at the gym and work off some of it. The treadmill, the cross trainer, the bench press.

Machinery that he hated. How he hated it. The associations were nightmarish, and the masked man knew it was the cruelest twist of all that he now had to use this equipment to stay fit and strong enough to do his all-important work.

He had to use all his self-control not to vandalize the machines. Not to throw aside the weights, topple over the treadmills, slash a hole in the fitness bands and Pilates balls.

And there were always women there, women in shorts, in sports bras, in tank tops. Fit, muscular: it made him burn with rage to be there in the same building with them.

But he would do it. He had to. He had to use the machinery at the gym, and he had to set up his next kill. He had to have a plan and stick to it. He knew he was good at what he did, and he knew he was clever. He'd get it right. He always did.

He wouldn't let his rage overtake him. He had to stay in control.

This was all about power, and he knew he was going to reclaim the power that had been so cruelly ripped away from him, all those years ago.

"Get that heart rate up! You're a lazy body. You're a lazy, useless, soft little couch potato. Make that heart work. I want to see it in the stratosphere!"

Body by body, mask by mask, he would set his own personal world to rights. In the bag, he could feel the wicked curve of the devil's mask.

This was the one he would use next, he decided. And by 'next' he meant 'now.'

It was time for the next kill.

CHAPTER EIGHT

When Connor pulled up outside Dirk Fisher's house, Cami saw immediately that it looked as if nobody was home. The house, a simple, single-story home wedged between other similar ones, was locked up tight with curtains drawn.

To make sure, Connor got out and banged on the front door.

He waited a minute, then banged again. No answer.

"He might be at work," Cami suggested, staring around the neighborhood. It didn't look like anyone nearby was home. This, she thought, was an area where people worked hard to raise their kids, and in the late mornings, there was nobody around. Kids and parents were all at school or the office.

"What work does Dirk do?" Cami asked, wondering if they could head there next.

"No record of employment," Connor said.

"No record at all? Not even a past place of work?" Cami hazarded. It was frustrating to her that the databases which police and FBI could access could be so helpful at times, but at other times, could yield nothing.

"I know. I feel the same way when they're not up to date. He might have changed jobs recently, or be doing something that pays him in cash rather than being on the record," Connor said. "Lots of reasons."

That didn't help them to know where he was. But then, Cami had an idea.

"Would it be worth going past this gym where he was caught lurking?" she asked. "I mean, he clearly spends a lot of time there, and a warning from the police might mean nothing to someone who has a murderous agenda. Maybe we should go and see?"

It wasn't far away. It wouldn't waste their time. And Connor clearly felt her reasoning was good. He nodded.

"Let's take a drive past. If he's obsessed with this, he might be there."

They were definitely looking for an obsessive personality, Cami thought, with a sick feeling as she remembered those rapid kills.

They got back into the car. As they drove to the gym, Cami took note of what a short way it was. This gym would have been his first stopping off point from his home, and he might have felt drawn to it. Perhaps as he gained confidence in his kills, he had broadened his horizons and gone further afield.

When they pulled up outside the gym, Cami saw it was a busy center that clearly specialized in wellness. The gym itself adjoined a medical aesthetics practice, doctors' offices, and a health food store along with a few coffee shops, clothing stores, and other businesses interspersed between them.

The parking lot was three-quarters full. People in tracksuits, gym gear, and yoga pants were walking briskly to and fro. As soon as Cami opened the car door, the sound of thumping workout music filtered through the air.

They would need to look around for a person who fit Dirk Fisher's description, Cami realized. Such a person might be trying to blend in, lounging in one of the cafés or juice bars, or simply standing around and checking his phone, waiting for a potential victim to walk out.

"Let's sit down," Connor said, obviously concluding that they needed to see the lay of the land.

Connor walked over to one of the juice bars and sat down at a table near the door that faced the gym.

"Water, please," he said to the waiter, without even looking, and put a five dollar bill on the table. Cami respected that about him. He'd never sit down for a minute without ordering something, and she had noticed he was always kind to waiters, doormen, and the people who stitched society's fabric together.

"So, show us what he looks like," Connor said, and Cami quickly called up the photo of Dirk on her phone.

He looked to be in his early thirties. He was clean shaven, with a narrow face, and a mouth that was set in petulant lines, Cami thought, though that could have been just a bad photo angle. His hair was brown, and although you couldn't see very well from the photo, his eyes were blue.

But he was an average person. There was nothing very remarkable about him. He could easily grow a beard, or put on a wig, and take on a totally different appearance.

"Maybe I should go into the gym, see if I can find him inside," Cami suggested.

"Let's wait for a minute," Connor said. "There's more likelihood of him being outside, if I remember the wording of that police complaint. If he's been harassing people, they're not going to allow him in, that's for sure."

Cami kept her eyes peeled. The waiter brought a bottle of water, and Connor poured them each a glass. Cami sipped, staring around, wanting to find him. She wanted to be the first to spot him, and to show Connor that even in this emotionally traumatizing time, she was on her game.

But of course, it was Connor who suddenly straightened up and said, "I see him!"

Cami's head whipped around as she stared in the direction he was looking.

Fisher had materialized seemingly from nowhere. He was standing outside the gym, and he had his back to Connor. But that dark brown, neatly cut hair was a clue, and now, so was the way he was hovering at the exit, as if waiting to pounce. His body language looked predatory, she thought.

Although he lived close enough to have walked here, he hadn't walked, she observed, as he was holding car keys in his hand and glancing back at a white vehicle that was parked nearby.

Maybe that was part of his chat routine. Come get in my car, I know a good workout place somewhere else. Or maybe he wanted to make a quick getaway if someone got angry enough. Maybe the women who got mad at him were the ones that he then targeted to kill. Cami didn't know what this killer would do to single out his victims, but clearly he had an effective method since three had died.

The car was electric. Out of habit, she ran her search program, to see if it could pick up that car's particular Bluetooth and network. It might be a waste of time, but rather spend the time than pass by an opportunity, she thought.

As she looked up again, holding her breath in suspense, he moved purposefully toward the gym's entrance. He was moving toward a slim woman, with her sweaty hair pulled back in a ponytail, who looked fit and toned and around thirty years old. She was walking briskly out of the gym.

Dirk Fisher was watching the girl, his head moving back and forth, as if he was trying to work out the right moment to approach her. And then, he did. He walked straight up to her and took her by the arm, grabbing her by her sleeve.

The woman turned to him, first looking surprised, then angry. Dirk was speaking rapidly and now he had an actual hold on her arm that looked more like a strong grip than a friendly touch.

And then, she started to look scared. She pulled away, and headed for the street at a half-run.

"Oh, no, you don't!" Now they heard Dirk's voice, loaded with intent. With purpose in every inch of his bearing, Dirk turned to follow her.

"It's time," Connor muttered.

He stood up from the table. Cami always felt amazed how a big, solid man like him could cover distance at such speed. Within a moment, he was tapping Dirk on the shoulder.

Dirk, who was a few paces behind the woman and gaining, stopped in his tracks. He looked around, just as Cami was rushing up to join Connor. She saw his face change. From the wheedling fake smile that was pasted in place, it tightened into an expression of horror.

"FBI. We need to speak to you urgently," Connor said shortly.

"I'm not speaking to you!" His voice was filled with defensiveness.

And then, he broke away, ducking from Connor's arm, and sprinting for the car that Cami had noticed earlier.

He jumped in, started it up, and veered into traffic. Horns blared and brakes squealed as he sped away.

Connor swore. "I didn't know he'd arrived by car. I thought he'd damned well walked."

"I saw the car earlier," Cami explained.

Connor stared after the speeding vehicle, and then glanced back at his own car, all the way around the corner in the parking lot.

"Looks like there's some traffic ahead. It might slow him. We can try and chase him down, and if he gets away, I'll put an APB out."

Cami glanced down at her phone. She wasn't expecting much at all. But her program had performed far better than she'd hoped.

It had not been able to hack into the car's electronics. That would have taken far longer.

But tacked above those good, solid pieces of coding was something else. Dirk had installed a cheap, shoddy alarm system in his car. Why, Cami had no idea. Why not choose quality, since you had a nice car to start with?

But the alarm gave her an in. If nothing else, the noise would startle him, but if it was wired deeper into the car's system, she might get more. And it was most definitely their last option for now, because the traffic at the light was already dissipating and in a moment, Dirk would be gone.

"Wait, Connor. I'm going to trigger his alarm and see what happens," Cami said quickly.

Hoping that it might cause a chain reaction which would slow this fleeing suspect down, she stabbed her finger down on the 'Alert' button.

CHAPTER NINE

Cami was hoping that something would happen when she activated the cheap, poorly coded alarm. Hopefully, it would be something that would slow Dirk's getaway, or better still, make him panic and jump out. And she wasn't disappointed. Immediately, the wail of a loud siren came from the car and the brake lights flashed.

"Good work. Can you do anything else?" Connor asked. "That's slowed him for sure."

"I don't know. Let me check."

Now, glancing down at the controls, she saw that the car alarm had an immobilization function. That hadn't been visible previously and she guessed her program was still working its way through the car's electronics roadmap. But if that worked, it would be very useful. Deafening as the siren was, he was still able to drive it. But perhaps not for long, if this next step worked.

"I might be able to. Hang on," she said. She didn't want Connor running in the wrong direction, back to his car, if this worked.

Quickly, Cami tapped the 'Immobilize' key.

And watched, pleased and surprised, as the car coasted to a stop.

"Nice work!"

Connor sounded amazed, but he didn't have time to say more, because he was already sprinting toward the stranded car. Inside, Cami could see Dirk was looking panicked. He was trying to restart the car. Then he began hitting the steering wheel with his palm in frustration.

"Wasting your time," Cami muttered, pacing forward, keeping an eye on her phone and another eye on the fugitive.

Too late, Dirk decided to run.

He wrenched open the car door and scrambled outside. But, as he did so, Connor powered the last few strides and reached the car.

He grabbed Dirk by the wrist and swung him around, so that he staggered, falling back against the car. For a moment, Dirk looked like he was going to fight. He was shouting. Connor was shouting back. Most likely, they needed to hear each other better.

Cami pressed a button, and the alarm stopped. Now, she hoped, Dirk could understand Connor nicely, because she was sure he was telling the other man important information. Like reading him his rights, she thought.

Putting her phone away, Cami jogged up to join them.

"You are under arrest for failure to obey a law enforcement officer, and also, we will be adding harassment charges to the list, if the police can make contact with the witness leaving the gym," Connor said. "It sure looked like you were harassing her, and that's after a warning from police to stop doing that."

Dirk was now looking appalled, as if he was starting to understand the extent of the potential trouble he was in. And they didn't even know what else it might include, Cami thought, staring at him sternly. At any rate, the fight seemed to have gone out of him. She thought that having his car blare a siren at him and then coast to a stop while he was getting away had been a major blow.

It was the typical behavior of a bully, Cami decided. Now that he was at a disadvantage, and clearly overpowered, he was buckling down and she guessed they were going to see a different side of him.

Dirk sighed. His shoulders slumped.

"Can I take my keys?"

"Sure."

"I didn't mean to do any of this."

"If you want to make up for what you've done, then you can cooperate fully during the questioning," Connor said, his expression not giving an inch.

Dirk leaned over into the car and got his keys. He glanced at Cami, looking briefly suspicious, and she guessed he was wondering if she, and her phone, had anything to do with the sudden failure of his car.

"Come on," Connor said.

He turned and trudged with Connor to the police vehicle, his demeanor now defeated and subdued.

They got in, with Connor making sure the car's back doors were locked so that they couldn't be opened from inside. Then they headed to the closest police department. Cami had to stop herself from glancing around at the suspect in the back seat, who was now shifting uneasily. She caught a glimpse of his anxious expression as they turned into the parking lot. She felt eager to know what Dirk's version would be, and hoped that he carried on in this cooperative frame of mind. She'd seen how sometimes going into an interview room seemed to trigger people's walls and defenses all over again.

This was the suburban police department that Cami was sure must have handled the complaint from the gym goers, since it was so close by. As Connor hustled Dirk out of the car, Cami wondered again if this harassment had been the precursor to bigger, more serious crimes. He looked like that kind of character. He was smooth looking enough to believe he was the answer to any woman's prayers, she thought, with a flash of contempt. And clearly, he had a creepy entitlement that had allowed him to justify this behavior in his own mind.

Cami climbed out of the car at the police department and Connor quickly processed Dirk, before leading him through to an interview room.

It was clear that at this local suburban department, the interview room wasn't often used. In fact, it had two spare desks with a few chairs stacked on top of them, stored inside. A couple of cops rushed through in a flurry of action, and moved the extra furniture out.

When the room was back down to one desk and three chairs, they filed inside and sat Dirk down in his position on the opposite side.

It was time for the questioning, and Cami felt a flare of hope that they might be sitting opposite the suspect, and that this crime might be solved soon. Right now, she was not in a mind frame to handle any more dead bodies.

But to her dismay, Dirk had done exactly what she hoped he wouldn't. He was looking defiant and uncooperative, as if now that he was face-to-face with the cops, he was ready for a last stand.

"So," Connor asked Dirk conversationally. "For how long have you been harassing women outside the gym?"

Dirk shrugged. "I didn't harass anyone. All I did was talk to her, and I don't see anything wrong with that. Women like to be talked to. I want a lawyer."

"You can have a lawyer if you like. Depends how long you want to sit here," Connor said.

"I want to go," Dirk grumbled. "You're harassing an innocent man."

"You were harassing innocent women. You were seen by a number of witnesses, including us, chasing women after they left the gym. That's against the law, you know," Connor told him.

"I don't know about any harassment," Dirk repeated, spreading his hands in appeal.

"You didn't notice that she deliberately told you to back off?" Connor asked.

Dirk shrugged again. "You know, I don't always take no for an answer. I mean, I was always taught not to take no for an answer."

"That's a very dangerous mindset, and you know it," Connor thundered. He looked genuinely mad at that comment, Cami thought.

Dirk looked at his hands, on the table in front of him, and wiped them on his shirt. Unconsciously, Cami thought, as though he were rubbing something off.

"Are you aware of the recent murders of athletes? Including two women who used to use this gym, and one who you harassed to such an extent she started carrying pepper spray?" Connor continued. "Both Lynne Horwood and Jill Whiteley have used this gym in the past, according to our records. Jill was one of the trainers here. Pepper spraying someone indicates a serious level of threat."

"Yeah, I saw that. It was on the news. I don't know anything about it. I mean, I have no idea who that killer could be. You're not saying I had anything to do with that, are you? Are you?" Dirk said, his tone suddenly high, with a hint of panic. Now, for the first time, he looked utterly aghast.

For sure, he had just realized why he was here.

But Cami still didn't know if the expression of pure panic on his face was because they had found him out as a killer, or because he genuinely wasn't the murderer.

"You've been harassing women, including regulars and trainers at this gym. So, you know, the way things look right now, that doesn't look good for you."

Connor frowned at him, and Cami could see that Dirk's anxiety was now rising.

"I didn't have anything to do with it, and I don't know anything about it. I'm not going to lie. I mean, I'm a guy, I like talking to women. But I would never hurt them or anything. You can't pin this on me. You can't." His voice was a higher register now.

"In that case, you'd better tell me your whereabouts last night, at around eight p.m. Give or take a couple of hours either side. Do you have an alibi?"

Dirk practically sagged with relief.

"Yes, I do. I do have an alibi for that time."

"Where were you?" Connor was clearly not believing a word he said without detail and proof.

"I was at work."

"What work do you do?"

"I supervise a team of office cleaners. I got the job a month ago. I'm a manager, you know," he said defensively, as if not wanting Connor or Cami to believe he was in a menial job. "We go on shift at five p.m. and we are usually done by around midnight. Yesterday we were working in two big office towers in the city center."

"You have witnesses for that time?"

"Yes, I was with my team the whole time. I was checking off the rooms online as they were done. And those buildings, they're secure places. You can't just come and go. We have to go past security to get inside. I'll show you my sign-in and sign-out, if you can pass me my phone."

He was babbling now in his anxiety to prove that he was not a killer. And, as Connor took his phone and looked over the time schedule, Cami guessed that he was seeing enough physical proof to confirm this.

She felt disappointed. They were still on the hunt. They'd caught a creepy harasser, but not a killer.

"We're handing you over to the local PD," Connor said, his voice hard. "They can take this further. No woman deserves to be harassed, and you already had one warning."

Looking angry, he got up and walked out, with Cami hurrying alongside.

While Connor was explaining the situation to the local police at the front desk, his phone began ringing.

He glanced down at it, and quickly stepped aside to take the call.

"Another one?" he said, in a tone that Cami instantly recognized, and which gave her a sick, helpless feeling.

They hadn't been in time. This murderer was on the loose, and he was picking off his victims with cunning and stealth.

Cami knew, now, the worst had happened. They were about to head out to view another murder scene.

CHAPTER TEN

With the devil's mask on the car seat beside him, the killer smiled. He was parked outside a luxury spa and gym, and he was waiting for the right moment. There was a lot that went into this. Planning, preparation, and of course, the raw courage and fitness that was needed to execute the crime. For this particular kill, timing was all important, because he knew he had a very narrow window.

It wasn't easy. It took all his focus, although in the background, he was playing his favorite music. Dark and threatening songs with a heavy beat, they spoke to the damaged parts in his soul and helped him remain calm.

This was the music he loved. Not like the music he'd been forced to listen to in the past, which was the music that you heard in every gym. Bland, canned tunes with a frenetic beat that were supposed to 'energize' but which had no depth, no meaning.

"I want you," he said aloud, looking up at one of the gym's large windows. This was the woman he'd earmarked as his next target, and he had to admit, he wanted to take her badly.

She was everything that he hated and despised.

She was super fit, and a physical overachiever who had a string of trophies and titles to her name. She didn't just practice fitness. She epitomized fitness.

There was nothing soft or curvy about her. She was all hard lines and toned muscle. She looked like a body builder, he thought disparagingly, and that was not at all what he preferred.

She had brown hair, which she often wore up in a tight ponytail, and which bounced vigorously as she sprinted on the gleaming treadmill, her face set in a determined expression, her gaze fixed on the screen where she could see her speed, her distance, her heart rate.

This woman never smiled at strangers. She was serious and withdrawn, and she didn't care for anyone who wasn't part of her elite fitness circle.

He thought about the day he'd first encountered her, which had been about a year and a half ago, when he'd first resumed his own fitness quest. She'd been outside the gym, sipping on a smoothie, chatting to her friends. They'd all been laughing as he had approached. It was the only time he'd ever heard her laugh.

He'd smiled at her, wanting to be polite, and she had actually turned away, and said something to her friends, who'd all laughed louder, and looked at him in a way that had made his blood boil with anger. Yes, he had been flabby and out of shape at the time, but that was no reason to mock a person.

He hated her for her fame, for her strength and for the way she walked through the world with the confidence of someone who knew no fear. She'd never been humiliated in public, like he had, he guessed. But she was quick to humiliate others.

She was everything he hated in a human being. Not only her body shape, but the mindset that came with it, which he loathed and scorned.

"You made your own future. Your actions have caused this," he reprimanded her.

His eyes gleamed at the thought she would finally be getting the punishment she deserved. He was going to make her pay for everything that she represented.

There were two other women in the gym at this time. He'd seen that they went in and out of the gym, sometimes with this fitness queen, and sometimes alone. They were not training partners, but they were friends. However, she trained some sections separately.

It was going to require a careful balancing act to find the moment when she was not with them. He'd waited here twice before and neither time had been successful. He hoped that today, things would align in a way that allowed him to get inside.

Of course, he might be seen even with his careful planning. In fact, there was always a chance of that, and he had to be ready.

But, he wasn't going to let fear stop him. He was good at what he did, he knew his capabilities, and he knew what he could get away with.

Right now, he was waiting for the moment he needed, when the receptionist who manned the gym's front desk would get up from her seat and go to the restroom. She usually did this a few times a day because she was an obsessive water drinker. Watching her chug back bottle after bottle of water made his own bladder feel as if it was straining. No doubt, she believed it had health benefits, but it had other benefits, too, that would help him. It got her out of her seat and away from her desk for a full five minutes. Five minutes was all he would need, if he could get the timing perfect.

46

Of course, he couldn't just walk in when she was there. That would be too brazen. He had to enter when she was nowhere around, and quickly pass through to the back of the gym.

And he had to do so at the moment when his target would be alone in the pool area.

She swam relentlessly for up to half an hour during these training sessions. He could only imagine how mind-numbingly exhausting it was. What a waste of effort. But so far, her swim had not coincided with the receptionist's bathroom break.

He wasn't going to rush this, he told himself. But then, he felt a rush of excitement as he saw the receptionist stand up and follow her well trodden path to the restroom. This was the moment. The two activities had aligned.

He put the mask in a gym bag.

Quickly, he walked inside, keeping his head down, vaulting cleanly over the turnstile that she was supposed to activate to let new customers through.

The slap-slap of the treadmills came from upstairs, but those were now the other two women at work. The one he wanted, his special target, was in the pool, straight ahead, behind the frosted glass doors that gave the swimmers privacy.

Futile, meaningless endeavor. What was the point of it? Striving to be faster, stronger than anyone else.

"You're just wasting your life. Do you really think this benefits society in any way?" he hissed angrily.

Part of him wanted to shout at her, to tell her that she was a waste of space, but that would be pointless.

She didn't care what anyone thought of her. She never stopped to talk to ordinary people. She most probably didn't even care about the skinny girl who worked at the front desk and who drank water like she was trying to drown herself from within. She only had interest in her friends, the ones who belonged to her elite circle. All she cared about was achieving those empty goals, and making herself better than the others.

Oh, he was about to shatter her world.

He stood at the frosted glass door, his eyes fixed on her. But she didn't see him. He watched her arms and legs move in a machine-like rhythm, as if she had been switched on and someone had forgotten to switch her off.

He felt a flash of triumph, because now she was in the state where he could get her. She was ready for him. After this long, multi-phase workout she would have exhausted herself, through this meaningless torture, to a level where the fight in her heart was gone.

He knew how that heart would feel. When he grabbed her he would be able to feel her pulse. Just like he had all the others.

It would be pounding, fast and strong and frenetic.

Thud-thud-thud, it would go.

And then, the killer gave a cruel, satisfied smile as he thought about how it would stop. He wondered what the reading would be, before the fitness watch showed the death throes and then finally flatlined.

He put on the mask and stepped through the door, his own heart rate accelerating as he anticipated the moment of the kill.

CHAPTER ELEVEN

Cami was already heading for the door as Connor got off his phone call and barked out a few last-minute instructions for Dirk Fisher to the local cops. She felt anxiety surge. This killer felt weirdly invisible to her. Who was he? Where was he now?

And how was he choosing these victims?

"Let's get moving," Connor muttered to her as he strode to the door. "The latest victim was found this morning. She'd only been at the gym an hour. He killed her in broad daylight."

Cami drew in a sharp breath, feeling stressed by this news, because it showed that this killer was gaining confidence. He was getting bolder. Killing in broad daylight. While other people were coming and going.

The only thing that Cami hoped was that he'd made a mistake. Surely he might have made a mistake, she thought, feeling stressed as she scrambled into Connor's car. He pulled onto the road and floored the gas pedal, his frustrated sigh telling her that he felt just as powerless as she did right now.

"The gym was open at the time. People were coming and going. The victim was alone in the swimming pool area, according to the police." Connor said, as he drove with ease, weaving in and out of traffic. "He clearly didn't have any problems with the threat of interruptions, or with other people being there."

Cami felt her pulse quicken.

"He must have watched for a while."

"Yes. I'm sure he did that."

"No witnesses?" she asked, feeling sick to her stomach.

"Not that I know of," Connor said, shaking his head.

"How did he get in without being seen?"

"We're going to find that out."

At the rate Connor was driving, Cami knew that they'd be finding out sooner rather than later. He wasn't wasting a moment in getting where they were going.

As they sped out of town, Cami was thinking frantically of how this killer could have done such a thing. How could he have gotten to this woman so easily. How had he known about her? And how had he killed her?

She wasn't buying the theory that all these victims had been scared, and nor was she convinced that this killer had somehow managed to push them past their limits. On a track, yes, maybe that would have been possible. But in a pool? That, she doubted. It wasn't as if this psychopath was going to chase them up and down the pool doing laps.

There must be something else he was doing. And she was sure that Connor was thinking the same thing, as he turned off the main road and sped up a side street.

Cami saw that this gym was in an upmarket suburb, located in an area of large homes, big yards, and spacious lots. When Connor pulled up outside, Cami saw that this gym was not just a fitness destination, but also a spa where customers could enjoy treatments, massages, and beauty therapies. There were ranks of luxury cars in the parking lot to the side of the building, but a lot of the customers were leaving, looking shocked and upset.

She noticed that there was a good view of the gym's lobby from outside here. You could also see the upstairs treadmills. Perhaps he'd just parked here and watched till he was ready to strike.

Three police cars were parked right outside the main gate, and Cami saw that a cop was standing at the main door, talking urgently on the phone.

As she scrambled out, Cami saw that the gym and spa had two different, signposted entrances. So if this killer had been targeting someone in the gym, then the spa customers would most likely not have known about it. She also couldn't see any cameras nearby, apart from one camera which was set to record car number plates of people using the main parking area.

Cami felt sure that the killer had known that camera was there, and had taken steps to avoid it. She didn't think they were going to get so lucky as to find his car's number plate, although she knew that Connor would check the footage carefully. But it was her bet that he'd parked outside, watched carefully, and then walked in through the pedestrian gate, which didn't have any cameras trained on it.

"FBI Agent Connor and Cami Lark," Connor said to the cop, who'd just finished his call. "Where did the murder occur?"

The cop pointed to the door signposted "Gym."

"In there, agents," he said, including Cami in the greeting. "There's a swimming pool at the back of the gym. That's where she was found, an hour ago."

"Any witnesses, anyone who saw what happened?"

The cop shook his head. "We've questioned everyone who was here at the time, but nobody saw or heard anything. She was training alone at the time."

Cami followed Connor inside.

There, she saw a receptionist at the front desk. The pretty, red-haired woman was looking shocked and upset.

"I didn't see him," she was saying to another of the cops. "I never saw anyone. I took a bathroom break for a few minutes, and now I think he might have been watching, and sneaked in then."

She looked tearful at the thought, and Cami knew with a flare of sympathy that she was blaming herself.

"FBI Agent Connor," Connor said. "Ma'am, did you notice anyone lurking outside the gym? Anything unusual today, anyone complaining about being watched or harassed?"

She shook her head. "It's always a quiet day today. But Rosanne Jeremy trains here most days, quiet or not."

Connor nodded. "So she was the victim?"

"Yes. She was such a great athlete. She was a pentathlete, and she used to practice her running, weight training and swimming here. She was hoping to represent the USA at the next Olympics, and now she's dead!"

She shook her head, tears flowing from her eyes.

Cami saw that this gym was large and spacious, with several different training areas, and a huge amount of equipment, even though in such a big space, it didn't seem crowded. There were windows everywhere, some overlooking the tranquil, well manicured grounds of the spa, and others overlooking the quiet suburban road and the parking lot with its planters and trees.

Cami guessed that with this big window in the reception area, it would have been easy for the killer to have stayed out of sight and wait until she'd left her desk. It would definitely not have been difficult to do that.

Now, they needed to view the victim, and see if this time they could figure out exactly what had happened.

"We'll go through and take a look," Connor confirmed, as Cami did her best to prepare herself. She remembered the words of Jacenta, the sharp, savvy agent who'd been assigned as her parole officer and adviser after she'd made her deal with the FBI.

Jacenta had told her that she must bring all her skills to this moment in a crime scene, because what she could pick up here might allow for this death to be avenged and for others to be prevented. It was a way of honoring the victims and making sure they did not die in vain, she had explained.

Cami kept that in mind as she and Connor pulled on their protective gear and headed through the now-empty gym, ready to see the place where the victim had died. This time, she told herself, she was not going to be scared, or allow herself to feel nauseous, or hang back, reluctant to look at the harsh truth of death.

She was going to be on top of her game, Cami resolved. She was going to find the evidence they needed. Somehow, in the sparkling blue waters of the pool where this ambitious athlete had died, there must be some answers to be found.

"We need to find evidence," Connor said, echoing her thoughts, and the purpose in his tone made her realize what pressure they were under. "It's a very recent murder and that makes it more likely we may find something here. Otherwise, he's winning. So let's keep our eyes and ears wide open, and make this the scene that brings him down."

CHAPTER TWELVE

As Cami walked through the gym, she saw that the indoor pool was separated from the rest of the gym by frosted glass doors. These were now standing open, and there was a knot of people inside. A body was lying on a gurney. Clearly, the paramedics had already removed Rosanne from the pool.

Cami saw the cops and other emergency staff gathered around the pool. Connor strode over to them, and Cami followed, her mind once again veering to Ethan.

Cami started to get that familiar feeling of unease, that feeling of being in the wrong place, at the wrong time, and her pulse quickened.

This time, she reminded herself that she was going to be strong, and she was going to do what she had to. She was not going to flinch away from this dead woman, who she knew must hold some secrets to the killer's MO. She remembered her deal she'd made with life. If she could be strong, if she could crack this case, then Ethan would survive.

Her thoughts veered back to her handsome love interest as they approached the cops, and Cami had to wrench them away, feeling emotional all over again.

"FBI," Connor introduced them briefly. "Who found Rosanne Jeremy's body?"

"One of the other customers," a uniformed woman, who Cami guessed was one of the gym managers, said, stepping forward. She spoke in a shaking voice. "One of our regular swimmers came in at about lunch time and headed straight for the pool. We heard her scream. She came back, and reported that a woman had drowned."

"Did she report this to you?"

"Yes, she did. I was upstairs at the time, preparing one of the rooms for a private class. I rushed downstairs immediately. We knew about these murders, and felt it was impossible Rosanne could have drowned. Plus, we saw there were signs of a struggle. Her bathing cap had come off, and there was a graze on her cheek. That number on her arm looked very strange, too. We called the police straight away."

"Any wet footprints? Any sign of him leaving? Surely he must have been wet, if he attacked her in the water?" Connor questioned.

That was a good question, Cami thought, but the woman shook her head.

"We didn't see any footprints heading out of the gym, but unfortunately, she'd probably been dead for over an hour before the next customer arrived. We traced the time back from the moment our receptionist went to the bathroom, as we guessed that's when he must have gotten in. So he had an hour to get away, and if there were some drips on the floor, nobody noticed in that time."

It was a gym, after all, Cami supposed. There were probably customers going to and from the pool and the spa continually. So the surrounding environment would not, unfortunately, give them any answers. Maybe the victim herself would do that.

Cami stepped forward. She took a deep breath, and looked down at the tanned, fit looking woman who was lying face up, the gurney still dripping water. She was wearing a black one piece swimsuit. She looked fit and toned. The graze on her face looked raw. Her bathing cap was still floating in the pool. The number on her forearm was scrawled in thick, black letters, clearly in permanent marker.

"189"

She had been attacked, Cami was sure of it. Was there anything that might be able to confirm the details of how?

On Rosanne's left wrist, she saw a fitness watch. This was what he'd used, she felt sure of it.

"Connor, look," she muttered. "Can I see if I can get into it? There might be information that could help us, apart from confirming that he's using the heart rate as his reading."

Connor shrugged. "Sure. I'm not sure what else it will tell you, but go ahead."

Cami set her program to run, casting around until it picked up the watch's Bluetooth. Then, her coding shot forward, testing the parameters, searching for a way past the device's basic, bottom drawer security.

"I'm in," she said.

She quickly navigated to the woman's vitals. Her heart rate, her breathing, her swimming speed. There was a host of data.

As Cami had expected, the data was rising steadily as the workout progressed. Rosanne had been pushing herself hard, swimming her heart out, and the stats were there to prove it.

But then, right at the end of the session, there was a spike in her heart rate, over and above the already high frequency of beats.

"I think that was when she saw him," she said, showing Connor her phone screen that now depicted the moment when Rosanne's heart had accelerated.

"Yes, that would be likely." Connor sounded intrigued as Cami scrolled on.

For another minute, the heart rate and breathing continued to spike, and Cami could imagine the terror that Rosanne must have felt during those last moments of her life. It was chilling to imagine what had played out, here in this pool.

Then, she frowned. The heart rate had subsided into chaos, with weak peaks and troughs that she'd never seen on a fitness device before. It looked as if the heart had gone into arrhythmia for a minute. And then the movement stopped.

"He caught her," she said, feeling horrified as she saw the sky-high heart rate, but no forward movement. This was when the struggle occurred, and it lasted about a minute before the arrhythmia set in. That was a long time, Cami thought. What was he doing in that time? Something to have caused that problem, for sure.

The heart had peaked at 189 beats per minute, before the arrhythmia began and the vitals disappeared. Heart rate and breathing fell off the chart soon after, Cami saw, while Connor was peering intently down.

"That's where her heart rate peaked," he muttered. "At 189. And then he did something to make it fail. Then he checked her watch, and wrote it on her arm. How did he stop it? How is he doing this?"

"How?" Cami asked, feeling extremely frustrated. What was this killer doing? How was he managing this?

"He reaches them. And he struggles with them and kills them, and notes the vitals." Connor muttered. "How, how is it happening? This time, I am going to find out."

Cami watched, feeling surprised and intrigued, as Connor picked up one of the woman's lifeless limbs and held it gently in his grasp. Leaning forward, he examined it carefully, looking all the way up and down, checking between the fingers.

Then he did the same with the other arm. She was impressed by the thoroughness with which he worked. It was clear to her that he was not going to let any tiny detail go overlooked.

He paused when he reached a tattoo on her bicep, looking even more closely at the inked skin, and Cami guessed that a tattoo would be a good place to hide something like a needle mark.

But not all the other victims had tattoos.

Finally, he moved to Rosanne's legs, and then her feet. He examined her toenails, and even lifted her swimsuit to look at her abdomen. Then, he was done.

"No sign of needle marks," he said at last.

Cami felt frustrated. The woman had been killed, somehow. Then her heart had stopped. The last thing she had seen had been the killer. Yet, there was no evidence of what had happened.

What if he was spraying something into their eyes, forcing a syringe up their noses, doing something like that? It might be very difficult to find evidence of that, she thought, feeling discouraged.

"Let's get her to the morgue, and check her out. The pathologist can do a full autopsy, and see what he can find," Connor said at last.

Cami felt a thump of disappointment. Connor's efforts hadn't gotten them anywhere. They were still no closer to finding out what had happened, apart from the fact that all the victims wore fitness watches.

Could the watches have been somehow programmed to kill them, she wondered suddenly. What if they had been jimmied to allow an electrical surge through?

But she shook her head. A watch wasn't equipped to do that. It couldn't produce such a killing charge, and even if it could, then the skin underneath would show signs. She was now veering away from what was possible, in her desperation to find answers, and was all the way into fictional territory.

But then, Connor turned back.

"Wait a minute," he said thoughtfully. "There's one place I haven't yet looked."

Cami watched, wide eyed, as he gently pried the victim's mouth open with his gloved hand. That made her feel sick, despite her best efforts at control, and she had to turn her face away because this was too much, too close, for her to deal with.

He murmured to himself, his voice low. She couldn't hear what he was saying, and she didn't dare ask. She could imagine the expression on his face, though.

Then he turned back to her, and she heard a new note of excitement in his voice.

"Look here," he said to Cami, and then addressed the other cops and the paramedics, too. "Look at what I've found."

CHAPTER THIRTEEN

Cami stepped forward, feeling hesitant about approaching the victim so closely, but forcing herself to be brave about it. She found that her curiosity was overpowering her fear. Connor was sounding excited. Now, the paramedics were also clustering around. The forensic officer who had been working nearby was approaching curiously.

"In her mouth. Under her tongue. Look here."

Cami narrowed her eyes, biting her lip unobtrusively, hoping that she would be able to keep calm and controlled as she stared down.

She drew in a sharp breath as she saw what was there. Connor was right. There, under the woman's tongue, was the definite pinprick mark of a hypodermic syringe.

Cami couldn't believe it. With his intuition, and his experience, Connor had spotted something that so far had even escaped the pathologist's attention in the autopsy. She felt a wave of serious admiration for what that must have taken. Perhaps looking at such a fresh body had helped him see it, she thought.

Now, at least, they had answers on the manner of death, and that was a critical step.

"That's how he's doing it. So, he's getting close enough to overpower them. By then, they're at the limits of their endurance thanks to the workout. They're exhausted and it's not easy for them to fight back. They try, of course. That we can see, from the bruises and the scrapes and the marks of a struggle, but he still manages to get that needle in. I'd bet he uses the same place every time. He's gotten it down to a fine art."

"What drug or poison would he use?" Cami asked.

Connor shrugged. "Something highly concentrated. Very fast acting. It's not my area of expertise, but now that we know for sure there is something being used, the coroner might have more of an idea what it is."

He pulled his phone out, took a close up photo of the injection site, and dialed the pathology offices.

"Agent Connor here. Is Dr. Links available?" he asked. He waited a moment. "Doc. We have another victim here, sadly. This one, I've found a needle mark. It's in the mouth, under the tongue. It might be the place he uses every time. Can you recheck the other victims? Then we can hopefully nail down the M.O. At least you'll have an idea of what it is."

Cami could hear the pathologist offering amazed comments from the other side, and agreeing to reexamine the others immediately.

"We've looked at this fitness watch. Because it didn't fall off her arm, we were able to see the complete progression of the heart rate. It looks as if it went into arrhythmia for less than a minute before death, after it peaked. There are a series of rapid but very uneven beats. Any ideas on what could have caused that?"

Seeing Cami was watching intently, Connor switched the call to speaker. Now she heard the pathologist's voice clearly.

"The poison that comes to mind is aconite," he said. "I've never personally seen a victim poisoned that way, but I've heard of other cases. It can be that fast acting if it's highly concentrated. The effects will be almost instantaneous. It will cause brief arrhythmia and then immediate heart failure."

"Can you screen for it?"

"Yes. We'll ask the lab to do a specific screening for any traces in the system."

"And where would you get hold of such a poison?" Connor asked.

The pathologist sighed. "These days, with the internet and the dark web, anything is possible. Aconite is extracted from a flowering plant that does grow in North America, so it would be available locally if you knew where to source it."

Connor thanked him, said goodbye, and cut the call.

Cami thought this had been a significant breakthrough. They now knew that the likely poison was aconite, and that the killer would have been able to source it on the dark web. That probably meant some IT knowledge. Enough to be able to browse anonymously and do a bitcoin payment to purchase a highly toxic poison.

With Cami walking alongside, Connor paced back toward the gym's entrance.

"We know that he is carrying syringes with him, and that he must have a supply of this aconite, if it's that. He's looking specifically for victims that are working out, and working extremely hard. Pushing themselves to their limits."

Cami nodded. "The readings on those two fitness watches were all the way into the red, even before he came along. And those were prolonged workouts."

"So he wants his victims tired. He wants them to be exhausted enough that they don't put up a bad fight when he attacks. He may have other reasons for choosing such top athletes."

"You think he has something against athletes in general?" Cami asked.

"He may," Connor agreed.

They left the gym, now silent and empty apart from one policeman and the manager, and headed back to the car. Cami saw to her surprise that it was already late afternoon. This case, called in mid-morning, had taken the whole working day. They had made progress, but reached no resolution. She felt determined to work on it for as long as it took.

Briefly, when she got into the car, she looked up aconite, wanting to know more about it. A quick search told her that the purple-flowered plant was also known as monkshood and wolfsbane. It had been used as a potent poison since ancient times, with the poison being most concentrated in the plants' roots and tubers. It was commonly used to poison arrows and spears.

Cami had absolutely no doubt that if she surfed the dark web, she could find a supplier of aconite in concentrations that would stop a heart. Like the pathologist had said, all things were possible today, thanks to the internet.

"What we need to know now is - why these victims? How is he choosing them?" Connor asked, glancing at Cami as he drove.

"Yes. Why these women? They've all been at different gyms and workout places. They're all pushing themselves to the limits, and are seriously dedicated athletes. So yes, there must be some method he's using to target them. I would assume that by the time he gets to the gym, he knows who they are."

"Yes. Let's make that assumption and see if we can work back from it. I think we must head back to the FBI offices for now, and when we're there, I want you to see if you can find his hunting ground."

Cami didn't want to wait for Connor to arrive back at the FBI building. She could make a start on that now. To begin with, she needed to access all the victims' names, and then take a look at where they interacted online.

She could do that in the car, with the case folder open beside her and her laptop balanced on her knees. Now that they weren't driving to a murder scene, but rather away from it, Connor was going slower, so she actually had time to press the keys. It was definitely a smoother ride.

But what could she find?

Four victims. That number was shocking to her. Already, four women had died. Murdered in the most brutal, terrifying way while working out. How had he known who they were? What twisted methods was he using to pick them? How were they getting onto his radar? Questions crowded her mind, and she hoped that she might be able to outthink him and pick up the method he was using.

Working in a thorough and logical fashion, Cami checked the victims online, one by one.

Lynne Horwood had been killed two weeks ago, and at the time, she saw, they had thought it was a heart attack, even though the signs of a struggle and that odd, scrawled number had left a question mark over that diagnosis, suspecting that an attack or crime incident might have contributed to her death. Only when the next victim, Jill Whiteley, died did the police and pathologists start to realize there was a pattern.

Lynne Horwood had been doing strength training, using weights and a stationary spin bike, and had been in a small private gym at the time, according to the case report.

What could she find about her online?

Looking her up, Cami realized to her worry that there wasn't much public information on Lynne at all. She didn't have a personal social media that was visible to the world. She only had the social media that her sponsors and team set up, and that was very basic, giving nutrition tips, race results, bike information, but nothing on where or how she trained.

Cami felt uneasy. In past cases she'd always found that the victims shared a lot of their lives on social media. It had made it easy to see how they could have been targeted or tracked.

But how was she going to research someone who was seemingly invisible online?

She tried the next one, Jill Whiteley. Jill at least had a social media profile but it was very closed and private. There was nothing to be gleaned from it at all.

The only public profile was the victim whose crime scene she'd attended, Davina Bright. Davina was more public about her activities and achievements, and had even posted about upcoming competitions and her 'journey' to try and qualify for the Boston Marathon. So, theoretically, a killer tracking her would have gotten the information he needed. But that didn't explain the others.

She barely noticed when Connor arrived at the FBI offices. Quickly, she closed her laptop, grabbed her bag, and headed inside, fretting over the two-minute delay at security, and feeling relieved once she was walking down the corridor to Connor's office.

She opened the machine again before she'd even sat down at his small round boardroom table. Hitching herself onto a chair she checked Rosanne, the most recent of the victims.

Nope. Rosanne also hadn't advertised her workouts anywhere that Cami could find. This didn't help her at all.

Connor was busy on his machine, typing in updates to the case, when Fraser arrived at the office door, looking stressed and rushed.

Immediately, Cami's heart clenched, wondering if this meant there was news on Ethan. But Fraser seemed preoccupied for a different reason.

"Connor, if you're here for the next half-hour, the mayor and his entourage have just arrived for a meeting, with two representatives from the President's Council on Sports, Fitness, and Nutrition. They want this to escalate. They're fielding major panic and media attention and they don't have answers. Can you come downstairs and update them?"

Cami felt the pressure bearing down as Connor got up and rushed out. These murders were starting to cause major waves, and rightly so. They were brutal and inexplicable, and she couldn't see where or how this killer was choosing his prey. Without knowing his hunting ground, it meant less chance of finding him.

She tried a few different searches, tried a few more ideas and hacks, but her searches were not giving her what she needed.

Frustrated, she glanced up from her machine as she sensed someone at the doorway.

It was Connor. Back again?

"What's up?" Cami asked. "Do you want me to come to the meeting?"

"No," Connor said, and his voice was gentler than she'd ever heard it. And his face was sadder than she'd ever seen it.

He closed the door and sat down opposite her, and Cami stared at him wordlessly.

She knew this was it. The moment she'd been dreading had arrived.

CHAPTER FOURTEEN

Cami saw a depth of emotion in Connor's eyes that shocked her. Was Connor blinking back tears? Surely not, but the mere fact this was even a possibility was making Cami's eyes flood. She'd tried to be so strong, all day; she'd done everything she could, but now that harsh reality was facing her, it felt as if all her defenses were crumbling around her.

"I'm sorry, Cami," he said, his voice rough and uneven. "The injury was too severe. His body failed him. Ethan passed away, ten minutes ago."

Her chest hitched. She gulped in a huge sob. And then, she was wailing with grief, crying uncontrollably, fighting for breath as she tried to expel an agony that she couldn't contain, that was burning her up inside, corroding her with grief and guilt and regret.

No! He'd had his whole life ahead. He was so motivated, so driven. So alive. So loving.

And now he was gone.

"I'm so sorry," Connor said, his voice breaking as he reached across the table to take her hands and hold them tightly in his own. "It's desperately unfair, Cami. He was a good guy. He was one of the very best."

His touch was comforting. It was as if she was able to absorb some of his strength and solidity, to help her stay upright and keep breathing.

"He should never have died," she choked out.

It wasn't what she wanted to say. She wanted to wail out that she was the reason. To tell Connor that if it hadn't been for her impulsive decision to go to that bar, her obsession with uncovering the truth about her sister, he would be alive. She was the reason he was killed.

And she thought that he sensed it.

"Remember that this was not your fault," Connor said firmly, his voice intense. "You did not pull that trigger. If you had the smallest idea this would happen, you would never have gone in there. Regardless of what you're telling me and what you're not, that's the truth. Isn't it?"

"It's the truth," she gulped.

"You are not the one to blame. Do not blame yourself. Fighting crime was the reason he joined the FBI. It was the reason he tried so hard." Connor paused, and then continued in a more thoughtful voice. "I don't know if you knew this, but he lost his younger brother when he was a teenager. He was caught in crossfire after a store robbery. The bad guys shot him. Ethan always used to say to me that it made him realize you had to get everything out of life, because the bad guys could be there at any time, and that was why he did what he did."

Even though Cami couldn't get any words out, Connor's words were filtering in. She was finding them strangely comforting. This was who Ethan was. He'd lost his brother. That must have been something he held very close and personal, because he'd never so much as hinted at this terrible loss.

But he had known life was short and fragile. He'd known that at any moment it could end. It could be cut short, and if you didn't want the bad guys to do that, then best you got into the trenches and fought them. He'd lived his life to the fullest. But he was gone. And there was nothing left of him but memories that, right now, were too painful to bear.

Her hands were trembling. She tried to blink back the tears, tried to breathe. Her lungs felt tight, her throat choking.

Blinking tears away, she searched Connor's face, and she saw the depth of his grief. The fact that he was crying too, that he was hurting, that he was trying to find the words, only made her wail louder.

Connor sat for a while. Gradually, Cami got control over her sobs. The box of Kleenex on the table had already taken punishment that morning, during her debriefing, and now she grabbed another handful. Wiping at the tears, she blew her nose, feeling that no matter what she did, the grief would not stop leaking out.

"It's time to go home," Connor said gently.

Cami looked up at him through swollen eyes. "Am I off the case?" she asked, hiccupping out another sob. It didn't matter now. Nothing mattered but this loss.

"We'll talk tomorrow," Connor said gruffly. "If you want to carry on, you make the call tomorrow morning. It's getting dark now. There's not much more we can do tonight with no leads. Get some sleep. We need to take some time, to come to grips with what happened. And I mean both of us," he emphasized. "If we want to come back fighting tomorrow, we need to take a few hours now."

"Alright." Cami groped for her laptop bag and staggered to her feet. She felt wrung out, and strangely dissociated, as if nothing really made any sense or had any importance anymore.

She barely realized that they were walking out of the office, down the corridor, and into the basement. It wasn't a long drive to MIT, but she spent it staring blankly out of the window, watching the city lights brighten, the evening traffic start to get busy, all signs of a world that was callously moving ahead, and which she suddenly found irrelevant.

She stumbled out of the car at MIT, managing to stammer out, "Thanks for the ride."

Connor just gave her a brief nod. There were no more words.

She walked inside, feeling like a zombie, shuffling upstairs, crashing into her room and slamming the door.

She collapsed on her bed, and for the next hour, all she did was cry her heart out. How could she ever atone for this? She'd placed Ethan in danger, and no matter Connor's comforting words, Cami knew the blame lay with her.

Eventually, she was roused by the ringing of her phone.

Feeling as if every cell in her body was in slow motion, Cami reached for it. She didn't think she wanted to answer, but when she saw that the caller was her parole officer, Jacenta, she found herself swiping right.

"Hi," she got out in a cracked voice.

"I'm so sorry, Cami," Jacenta's musical voice sounded subdued and sad. "This is a tragedy nobody should have to go through. Nobody. How are you doing?"

"I'm shattered. I don't know what to do."

"I know you cared for him. You were close. He told me how much he admired you."

"He did?"

"Yes. He felt you were one of the most talented people he'd ever met. He hoped that you'd work here full-time. He told me that in confidence because he didn't know how you felt about joining the FBI. I know he liked you, and not just as a colleague. He felt a connection with you."

"I felt that too."

"Whatever happened is not your fault. Don't allow yourself to take responsibility for someone else's criminal actions," Jacenta said firmly, echoing what Connor had said earlier. "You can't protect anyone from the kind of thing that played out there, in that bar. You have no idea what the background was."

There was a meaning in Jacenta's voice that caused Cami's eyes to widen. It was almost as if she, somehow, knew something about that background. But she wasn't saying.

"You need some rest. And you need to look after yourself. I'm sending something your way. You take time, as much time as you like. If this case goes on without you, that's fine. But if you feel better tomorrow morning, then you take the day as it comes. Alright?"

"Alright."

"I'll call you and check in tomorrow. It's a terrible thing that happened. I'm so sorry, Cami," she said again.

Cami cut the call. For a few moments she stared into space, blankly, feeling utterly bereft.

And then, there were swift footsteps approaching the door, and a sharp, loud knocking. Cami jumped, all her adrenaline surging again. What was this? She felt unprepared to cope with anything at this stage.

Approaching the door cautiously, she opened it a crack and peered out.

CHAPTER FIFTEEN

Cami felt astounded that she was face-to-face with a young woman she didn't recognize at all, but who was wearing an FBI cap and jacket. Her skin was tan, her eyes were sharp, and she was holding a paper bag in her hand.

She didn't look much older than Cami.

"Cami Lark?" she said.

"That's me," Cami said.

"I've brought you a delivery, from Jacenta. You should be expecting it?"

"I - I haven't been expecting anything that has happened today," Cami admitted. "I think she mentioned it."

She stood aside, and the other woman paced carefully into the small room, and put the bag down on Cami's desk.

"Jacenta said you'd probably want to be alone now, but if you need her, you must call. At any time," she emphasized.

"Thank you," Cami said.

With a friendly nod on her concerned face, the woman quickly left. Too late, Cami realized she hadn't even gotten her name. She'd been feeling too shredded to have done that. But it had seemed as if she was briefed on Cami's circumstances.

Cami opened the packet. There were a few things inside.

A photo frame was the first thing she took out. Tears sprung to her eyes. Jacenta had thought that maybe there was something she might want to put in it, and there was. The photo of herself and Ethan, taken at a recent local metal band performance, was one of the most treasured shots on her phone. She could print it, frame it, and keep the memories.

She then pulled out a bottle of calming shower gel, with a strong lavender fragrance. Next was a pair of socks that looked soft and warming, followed by a packet of salty snacks, and another of chocolate cookies. Comfort food, comforting gifts. Small things that made a big difference.

Jacenta's kindness lanced all the way into Cami's heart. She felt amazed that someone she barely knew and had spoken to only a handful of times, had thought of being so caring as to bring her these small but important gifts. Her empathy and generosity astounded Cami.

In a strange way, it made her feel less alone in her grief, and as if there was going to be a path out of this, even though it felt like a hard and impassable road.

And it reminded her that within the FBI, Ethan had not been the only good person. He was the one that had changed her mind about the organization. But now she was beginning to realize how deeply everyone in the Boston office cared for one another. There was more than just a superficial camaraderie. In a career where death and injury was a real possibility, when fighting crime - even after hours, as recent bitter experience had taught her - the bonds were strong, and she was surprised to feel a part of them.

The organization was grieving. People were comforting one another. And Cami was among them. She was a part of them.

She texted Jacenta a quick 'thank you so much.' Then, feeling shattered, she took the shower gel to her tiny shower cubicle and had a fragrant, hot shower. After her shower, utterly exhausted, she collapsed into bed. She felt as if she was done with the day, as if there was nothing left that could possibly play out now.

But even so, a moment before she fell asleep, Cami had a sudden thought that penetrated all the way through the sleepy, battered confusion in her mind.

She had an idea about the victims, and how to find them. It had come to her in a stroke of inspiration. Cami couldn't ignore it. Exhausted as she was, she had to find out if it would be viable. She needed to search deeper, search using their private information, and look for a group that was focused on athletic prowess. If she did that, she hoped that she might find a place, at last, where they'd all interacted. Because for sure, they were sharing information somewhere online.

Feeling as if she was struggling with leaden eyelids, she unpeeled her face from the pillow, opened her laptop, and set out to see if it might get her somewhere.

***

The next morning, at seven a.m., she called Connor. She'd been awake since five a.m., working further on the theory she'd had the night before. She felt wrung out, but at the same time, she knew this research was solid.

He answered after two rings, his voice grainy.

"Cami? What's up? You okay?"

"I'm okay," she reassured him. "Connor, I've had an idea. About the case."

"You have?" Did she hear a note of respect in his voice? She thought she might have.

"Yes. I was trying to think outside of the box, and I came up with something."

"What idea?" Now his voice was sharper, as if he, too, was regaining much-needed focus.

"I thought I'd go deeper into where these victims interacted." Reaching into the bag of cookies Jacenta had sent, Cami picked out one, thick and chunky and studded with chocolate chips. She'd eaten two last night while researching, and one this morning before calling Connor. And she had to say that Jacenta was right on the money with her comfort food. Her brain had been screaming for sugar, which the cookies had provided.

Her grief was still there, like a powerful current ready to drag her down, but for now, her resolve was keeping her afloat.

"What did you find?"

"I was battling," Cami admitted. "Eventually I went really deep. I did a search using their phone numbers, their private email addresses. I was looking for somewhere more technical that they might share information like workout time, distance, heart rate and so on. And I found a group that they were all members of online."

"And what is it?"

"It's a forum that is actually more like a leaderboard, in that it's very focused on results and performance. It's private, and members only, but I found a way in. It's linked to their fitness devices, and allows them to post their times, their personal bests, their accomplishments."

"And they all used it?"

"They did," Cami said. "It's not a very nice site. It's not friendly. It's ultra competitive. This is purely a place for people who feel they've achieved something special to brag, and because it's linked to technology, they can brag without feeling that they are lying, I guess."

"So they all bragged on it?"

"They all posted regularly when they achieved good times or good results. And everyone posts their heart rate, all the time. I think it has to be linked to this, surely.

"Interesting. So you reckon he knows about this online forum? He follows this?"

"Yes. I think he does. He might even be a member of it. And I'm wondering if he might have been someone who got on the wrong side of these people. Maybe he didn't achieve what he thought he had, and then they belittled him when he tried to brag. That happens often here."

Cami looked again at the comments. Some of them were sincerely admiring, but only if the people listing their times had genuinely achieved something. Otherwise, the comments were downright cruel. They were nasty.

And she hated to say it, but all four of these women who'd been targeted by the killer had indulged in that nastiness. None of them had held back when someone had posted a substandard time, or had seemed to be lacking in fitness.

A man who'd come on here looking to achieve, hoping for praise, and who had been taunted and ridiculed instead, might have gotten very angry, Cami reasoned.

"That sounds like a solid lead. Can you narrow it down?"

"I'm working on it as we speak. I have programs running that are looking for people who fit the description. I don't know how many hits I'll get, but I should have something in the next few minutes."

"Keep it running," Connor advised. "I'll be on my way to pick you up in ten minutes."

Cami felt a wash of relief. She was still part of the team. She was still on the case. Connor needed her.

"I'll be ready," she assured him.

She hung up, feeling a lot better. A tiny bit of her grief was lifting, and she didn't know if it was because she had a plan, or because she felt she was getting somewhere.

Even though she was only one cog in the wheel, feeling that wheel turn had to alleviate her sense of helplessness.

And then, her program finished running and flashed up the results.

Quickly, Cami grabbed her laptop and took a look at what was there, reading through the profiles that her software had singled out.

Her eyes widened as she reached the third one on the list. She read through the info and then re-read, checking all the details such as location, address, time on the site, and comments made.

"I hope you get here quickly, Connor," she muttered. "Because I might just be looking at our killer."

CHAPTER SIXTEEN

The skull mask was the one he would use next, the killer decided. Because, to him, it emphasized everything he'd been through. The enforced denial. The feeling of being pushed to his limits. He'd often thought of himself as being nothing more than bare bones, without any strength, without any living flesh. Everything stripped away.

The killer stopped his car and parked in a secluded spot. There, on top of the hill, was his next destination. That was where he was headed, and this was a kill that had intense significance for him. He wanted to relish every moment of the experience.

As he stared at his faraway target, he heard the pounding of feet from behind him. He spun around, frowning as a woman in her forties jogged by. She was in the mold he hated. He saw that immediately. She was fit, strong, and focused. She glanced at her fitness watch as she passed him, causing him to tense in anger.

How he hated these women who pursued the goals that he'd been forced into.

They'd been born as athletes, and it showed in the way they moved. It showed in the way they thought. How he hated them for being able to do what he couldn't.

The skull mask was a reminder of how they had made him feel. Seeing their faces, seeing their bodies, hearing their voices, taunting him, and ridiculing him.

It reminded him of the words he'd been made to suffer during those torturous sessions.

"You'll never be an athlete. You'll never even be a man. Look at you. You are puny, weak, and pathetic. Look at this heart rate? Unacceptable! And why can't you chin the bar five times? You should be able to do it ten times!"

The voice had never gone away. That loud, taunting, bullying voice had stuck in his mind for years, as if lodged there immovably.

Every time he looked in the mirror he was reminded of those scathing criticisms. "Look at you. You're so skinny and bony. Your arms are like a rag doll's. That's what you are. You're nothing better than a girl. Only when I look at the girls that work out with you, they

71

are all fitter and stronger than you. Better speed, too. You're eating their dust, that's all you're doing. Just eating their dust!"

And he'd been insulted like that in front of the girls. His tormentor had never shied away from humiliating him in public. Not once had the girls been kind, he remembered. Those women, lifting weights, running on treadmills, seeking to smash their fitness goals, had been nothing but insulting to him. He'd never received sympathy or even help from them.

He had never been able to understand why his tormentor was so cruel to him. He had never been able to understand why he had made him lift weights that were way out of his league in terms of his body's strength, while taunting him when his heart hammered in stress and panic. He knew he didn't have the strength in his arms or his hands. They knew he wasn't strong. And yet he had made him try and try, and each time he'd ended up collapsed on the floor, in pain and humiliation.

"I hate you," he said.

He'd never said it at the time. He hadn't been able to summon the courage he needed to say those words. Like, "I refuse." That, too, had not been something he'd found himself able to spit out.

Instead, he'd buckled down and pushed himself to the limits.

Breathless, aching, nauseous, and under the iron rule of a man for whom his achievements would never be good enough.

"Your sister's doing better than you! She's managing a full set of reps. And she's a year younger, twelve pounds lighter, and five inches shorter. What's wrong with you?

He'd been too breathless to gasp out his reason, that he simply couldn't. That he didn't have the strength left in his body to continue, that he was still too young, that this was too much for him.

"I'm going to make you into a man," his tormentor had threatened. "Whatever it takes. You are weak and flabby and useless. Not a man to be proud of. I'm ashamed of you. Now try harder and show me what you're made of!"

He'd always been too weak to resist.

Those sessions had left deep scars in his psyche. And for years, after he'd left home, he'd rebelled.

With a frown, as he started to walk up the hill toward his target, he remembered how unfit he was. Now, the walk was easy for him, and he barely noticed the incline of the steep hill, even though he was walking fast. Back then, he wouldn't have been able to make it. At the height of his rebellion, he'd become that man sprawled on the couch in front of the TV, stuffing snacks into his mouth, rebelling against the years of misery.

Although he'd taken escape in that for a few years, he had not found that it healed him. In fact the scars had become even more raw and agonizing with time.

Then, one day, as he'd been heading for the grocery store to stock up on snacks, he passed by a woman who reminded him of all the ones he'd been taunted with as comparisons. She was fit, lean, and wearing gym gear. Standing by her car, she'd given him a look of utter contempt. As he'd lumbered past, she had sniggered.

And, in that moment, he understood what he needed to do to get true payback. He understood what was needed, but in the same breath, he realized that it would take planning and change to achieve it.

He'd go back to the gym, but this time, he wouldn't be the one who was weak. He'd become the one who was strong. He knew that to do what he now dreamed of, he would have to become the person he had hated and resented. Strength was necessary. Endurance was essential. And, most of all, he needed the total focus of a top athlete.

To fight them, he needed to be on equal terms.

And so, with revenge in mind, he'd set about his plan to get in shape. He'd begun his long journey. It had taken a year of going to the gym five times a week, and another year of lifting weights to get his body in shape, as fit and strong as he needed it to be. He'd done it the hard way, and he'd had to change everything about him. Except for the way he felt inside. That would never change. He wasn't proud of his strong, lean body, and in fact he considered it just an outward symbol of the inner pain he had felt for so long. He couldn't wait to destroy it, day by day, to erode it away all over again, sprawled on the couch in defiance.

But he couldn't do that until he had achieved his last and most important goal. This was the one he had been building up to all this time. Just as one might build up to a level of fitness, he thought, with a wry grin at that analogy.

He couldn't wait any longer because there was surely a chance that this next victim might realize the pattern in place, and that would mean that all his efforts had been wasted.

He needed this victim to be there, innocent and unaware, ready for him to arrive, and to receive the punishment for all those years of pain.

The killer smiled as he strode along, checking his pockets to make sure that he had the equipment he needed. It wasn't much, and it was easily concealed. Just one small syringe and a marker pen. That was all he had to carry.

So much easier than a full set of weights. And so much more effective, too.

He couldn't wait to use them.

CHAPTER SEVENTEEN

Cami was waiting outside the main gate of MIT when Connor arrived. She scrambled in the car, feeling utterly drained from yesterday, but with a steely determination about what today would bring. This chat forum held the answers, she was sure of it. It was the killer's hunting ground. It had to be.

And on it, she'd found a man who had a strong motive for murder.

"So, who's the suspect?" Connor asked. Glancing at him, Cami saw that he looked as if he was also short on sleep. She guessed that last night hadn't been easy for him, either. She could imagine how he would have had to notify his team, talk to Ethan's parents, manage this entire tragedy all while suffering his own grief.

But now, he was trying to put it aside, just as she was.

"There's a man on the site called Nolan Webster," she said. "He was a weightlifter who had Olympic dreams. He trained at the same gym as Davina Bright used, and I see that he was criticized by all four victims, as well as a lot of other people, when he tried to brag online."

"Why's that?"

"They said they thought his readings were false. That nobody could achieve what he'd achieved, with such a short time in training," Cami explained.

"How did he respond to that?"

"Aggressively. He's a very aggressive man. And as it turns out, they were right."

"They were? How?"

"He was kicked off the state team for using illegal steroids and fitness enhancers. At any rate, that's what one of the commenters accused him of. I then found a related news article that said he'd physically attacked his coach."

"Does he have a record?"

Cami shrugged. "I think he must. He was definitely arrested after the incident with his coach. I had so many search windows open by then, and this search took so long, that I didn't have time to check."

"I can ask the office to confirm. Do you have an address for him?"

"Yes. He lives in a neighborhood south of the city, and it seems that he is employed by a local gym."

"Let's head there now," Connor said. "What does he look like? You have a description?"

"Here's his photo," Cami said. "He's thirty five years old, six-foot-two, dark-haired."

Nolan was clean shaven, with a dark buzz cut. His tanned face looked hard and aggressive, a reflection of his personality, Cami thought.

After glancing at the photo, Connor pulled onto the road, and they began a stop-start journey in morning traffic, heading out of the city. As they inched their way through the traffic, Connor got on the phone.

"I'm looking for a record," he said to someone in the office. Someone who, Cami remembered with a pang, would have been Ethan if this tragedy hadn't happened.

"Name of Nolan Webster," he said. "You can text me the details. We're on our way there anyway, so it's just for background."

Cami watched out of the window. The day was gray and starting to rain, and the gloomy weather reflected her mood whenever she thought about Ethan, which was all the time.

She glanced at Connor's map display, seeing that they were almost at their destination now. They had reached an outlying suburb that Cami thought looked to be on the rough side. It was comprised of small houses and tall apartment blocks, nestled by the side of the railway tracks.

"The gym should be along this road."

Cami saw the signage for it almost immediately. A large, faded, black and white notice board was displayed above a big square building that looked like it could be a repurposed warehouse.

"Fight Club?" she said aloud. "Wonder who came up with that name?"

"At least it's giving us a clue," Connor agreed cynically.

The tagline below the name read, "Boxing, Fighting, Wrestling, Hand to Hand Combat."

Outside were a few motorcycles and a bunch of muscle cars. Cami had a feeling that there weren't going to be many women in this gym. In fact, she thought she could sense the excess testosterone already filtering out of the windows.

It occurred to her that since this killer had targeted only women so far, perhaps he felt more comfortable training in a place where there weren't any women. Maybe that meant that his lethal instincts were suppressed in working hours, she thought with a shudder.

Connor was checking his phone as he climbed out.

"Yup," he said. "Nolan has a record. A year and a half ago, for assault. He spent a month inside after breaking his coach's arm in a fit of rage. It should have been longer, but he pleaded in mitigation that steroid use had made him uncharacteristically aggressive. I see here he claimed it was legal use, though. But he could have access to other toxic substances and poisons, if he is linked into an illegal supply of performance enhancers."

He hurried to the gym's entrance, ducking his head against the worsening rain.

Cami suspected that even without steroids, Nolan might be characteristically aggressive. She couldn't help feeling nervous as she walked up the three shallow concrete stairs to the gym's main door. It was battered, as if some of the fights had overspilled the interior and ended up damaging it. Its handle was loose and rusty. Connor opened it and they stepped inside.

The space beyond was big and cold. Shouts and yells echoed off the walls. The floor, lined with faded linoleum and rubber mats, was divided into different sections, where pairs and groups of men were practicing combat maneuvers, wrestling, lifting weights, or attacking punching bags. A clanging sound came from somewhere and the place smelled of damp.

Cami had been right, she saw. This was an exclusively male environment.

At the reception desk stood a tall, broad-shouldered man in shorts and a muscle-shirt. He had a thick neck and a shaved head, and was so muscular that he looked as if he could lift the entire desk above his head.

"FBI, here to see Nolan Webster," Connor said. "He works here, I believe? We're looking for information from him regarding a case."

The man gave him a level stare, and Cami instantly picked up that he had no love for the cops.

"I don't work here. I just train here," he said rudely. Then, he shouldered his way past them and headed out into the rain.

Connor gave a sigh.

"I guess we head in on our own then. Might be better," he muttered.

He paced into the gym, looking around him.

Immediately, Cami saw, there was a combative atmosphere. Everyone paused in their hand to hand fights and weight lifting, to give Cami and Connor deeply suspicious looks.

"Nolan Webster? Where is he?" Connor tried, as he passed a fighting pair, but they simply stared at him in an aggressive way.

"What are you doing in here, baby?" someone said from behind Cami, in taunting tones. She spun around, but couldn't see who'd spoken. Then, from another direction, she heard a low, insulting catcall.

Connor, ignoring it, was striding toward the back of the gym, and she saw that he had at last spotted Nolan. He was with a client, a man who looked like he might be a professional fighter. They were dancing around each other, fists at the ready, and Cami could hear the harsh gasps of their breathing and their grunts of aggression.

Nolan had a twisted, sneering expression on his face, and he was holding his arms high, fists clenched, his height and reach giving him a big advantage over the other man. Then, with a cry, he attacked, and Cami could see that he was punching and kicking his opponent with a ferocity she'd never seen before.

"Hey there!" Connor waded in and began shouting at the two men, clearly trying to break up this vicious fight.

She took a step forward, trying to see how she could help, but someone grabbed her arm from behind.

"Hey, baby," the man said. His breath smelled of stale beer, and his skin was sweaty. When she tried to shake him off, he held tighter.

"Let go of me," she said angrily.

"What are you doing in here, baby?" he said again, mockingly. "You shouldn't have come in. This isn't a place for women," he said. "I don't think your boyfriend would like it if he saw you wandering around without him."

This time, Cami really did manage to wrench her arm away.

"Get off me!" she said, but he simply gave a disparaging laugh and headed back to his weights.

Connor hadn't seen this confrontation, which Cami felt relieved about, because it had been humiliating for her. He was looking ahead, focused on his suspect.

"FBI here! It's time for this fight to stop!" Connor called out to Nolan. "I want to speak to you. Urgently!"

But Nolan, who had clearly noticed them too, didn't stop. Refusing to break off his attack, he launched a punch at the boxer, who blocked it. Then, he got another, harder blow in, and the other man reeled back.

"FBI!" Connor shouted.

Nolan turned and spat out an evil curse in their direction, before resuming his destruction of his opponent, who was now down on his knees, head bowed, arms raised protectively.

Connor stepped forward and grabbed Nolan by the shoulders, hauling him up and off his opponent.

"Let him go," he said. He swung him around and faced him angrily. Immediately, Nolan raised his fists, looking savagely intent, and Cami flinched. She could see the raw aggression in his eyes. He was going to attack Connor. This was all going to happen too fast for anyone to control the damage.

Thinking of Ethan, she felt terrified this was going to end in disaster.

CHAPTER EIGHTEEN

Cami watched, holding her breath, as the two men stared each other down. Nolan looked ready to attack, but perhaps there was something in Connor's demeanor that was giving him pause. They were a heartbeat away from violence, that was for sure.

"You guys are here to arrest me? I'll go down fighting," Nolan suddenly roared. "Get off me! Get out! Now!" He took a step forward and Cami gasped, forcing herself to stand her ground, waiting to see how Connor handled it.

She didn't think that any sign of weakness would be well received. In fact, if Connor stepped back, she thought it might just light a fuse. She was aware that, behind her, some of the other men had stopped their workouts and were forming a rough circle, standing a few yards away.

Would he have time to draw his gun, she wondered. For some reason, she didn't think drawing a gun would be a wise idea now.

Connor didn't reach for his gun. He didn't show a moment's hesitation, or the slightest trace of fear.

"Touch either of us, and you're in jail," he threatened Nolan. "Didn't like it there last time, did you? Then don't sign up for a return visit."

Nolan's face twisted with fury, and for an instant, he seemed like he was going to ignore Connor's warning. Breathing hard, he bunched his fists. But then, he lowered his hands.

It seemed like the tension in this room eased just a fraction, although Cami could still hear one of the men whispering to her, almost inaudibly under his breath, from behind.

Resolving to be like Connor, she didn't give him the satisfaction of knowing she'd heard.

Just as she'd thought the situation was going to calm down, and Nolan was going to comply, the big man's temper surged again.

"It's private property. I won't have you here!"

In a sudden, violent move, he drew his right hand back and swung a punch at Connor.

Cami was sure he was going to knock Connor to the floor, or at least to the wall behind him. But Connor was ready, and Cami couldn't believe the speed and expertise with which he reacted. He blocked Nolan's punch and then, in one swift movement, he twisted Nolan's arm up behind him, and pushed him hard against the wall.

Nolan looked as shocked as Cami, as if he'd never expected an FBI agent to come back with such sharp, aggressive, and effective moves. Cami felt stunned by his technique. *Did they teach that at the FBI academy*, she wondered. It was so quick and effective that it made Nolan seem like a raging amateur by comparison.

Nolan was struggling and Cami could see that his face was crimson with rage and pain.

Connor was struggling too, but as Cami watched, he got the handcuffs on one of Nolan's wrists, and then clamped them over the other. Cami felt a surge of relief that this man was now under control.

"Hey!" one of the other men shouted, lunging forward and clearly keen to defend Nolan, but his fighting partner grabbed his arm.

"Let them sort it out," he muttered. "No need to get involved."

With Nolan now held at a disadvantage, the onlookers were turning away. They had wanted to see the cops beaten up, Cami realized. Watching Nolan effectively stumped by a clever technique was not what they had hoped to see. Now, these fair weather allies were making themselves scarce again, drifting off to the corners of the gym.

"I'm not going to let you go," Connor said through gritted teeth, hanging onto the cuffs. "One more wrong move from you, and you're going to be spending a long time in jail. You should already be there for attempted assault. I'm being kind," he threatened.

"I'm not going to make any wrong moves if you leave me be," Nolan warned, breathing hard and flexing his shoulders uncomfortably. "I'm not in trouble with the law this time."

"You might be. It depends on your answers to our questions," Connor said.

"If you're going to ask me questions, then do it outside. I'm not talking in here."

Cami narrowed her eyes. She didn't like that line of thinking, and thought it was very possible that Nolan might be planning on making a run for it, despite the cuffs. Connor obviously thought the same.

"It's raining outside. And it's a big wide world out there. I see a back office in this gym. Why don't we go in there?"

He indicated a door at the back of the gym.

"I'm not going in there with you," Nolan said. "You've got your gun. You're going to arrest me. I'm not stupid. I can see you're looking to frame someone. You provoked me into trying to attack you. This is a set-up."

Cami shivered. She didn't like the way Nolan looked at her. For a moment, she thought he was going to lunge at her. She wondered briefly if he was back on the steroids, because for sure he was aggressive, and also not coherent in his responses.

"Let's go into the room," Connor repeated calmly. "Just a few questions. If you're not the person we are looking for, then you can go."

This time, with an angry shrug, Nolan capitulated.

"I'm not that person," he muttered.

Connor grabbed hold of the cuffs tighter, and pushed Nolan ahead of him, going into the office. Once inside, Cami closed the door.

It was a basically furnished place, with an old broken punching bag on the floor, a battered desk, and three plastic chairs that didn't look up to the job of supporting the weight of the average heavily built gym customer.

Connor pushed Nolan down into one of the chairs. It seemed to creak and give under his weight, but it didn't break.

"Stay there," he said firmly, taking a position in front of the closed door.

Cami perched on another chair, glad to stay under the radar. Now that she had a chance, she wanted to see if there was anything she could access via Bluetooth.

Connor was now interrogating Nolan.

"You were criticized online recently, on the fitness website."

He shrugged. "Yeah. Some of the women on that website are witches."

"They accused you of steroid use, and you were then found guilty of it."

"That was Lynne Horwood. She thinks she's so famous, doesn't she? There was no way she could have known that at the time, and I'm going to bring a lawsuit against her," Nolan insisted. "That was defamation. She could have ruined my reputation as a trainer."

"But you were using steroids."

"Legal ones!"

"Really? Where did you get them? Off the dark web? Did you buy anything else while you were on there? Because we suspect a specific poison was used in these murders," Connor pressured him.

"The steroids were prescribed! The whole story got twisted. I lashed out in anger. I wasn't kicked off the team for steroid use, I was kicked off for getting mad at my coach. He didn't have faith in me. You've gotta have faith in your team! And Lynne is going to pay for it, you watch. Let me out of these handcuffs," he insisted, his face now turning red.

Cami was interested to see that he was referring to Lynne in the present tense. It was as if he didn't know she was dead, she thought, feeling confused. Connor had clearly also picked that up.

"Are you aware that Lynne was murdered recently?" he asked.

"I don't know anything about that," Nolan said, now sounding taken aback. "Are you serious?"

"Yes," Connor said.

"What happened? Did she try to bait someone else who didn't have my patience? I can see she had it coming!" His rage was surging again.

"She was killed while at her gym." Connor was watching Nolan intently, Cami saw, glancing up from her phone.

"I know nothing about that. I thought she deserved payback! But I wasn't going to kill her. Do I look stupid? I was going to sue her, but I haven't been in contact with my lawyers for a week. And I don't go online much, especially after those witches attacked me. I'm not interested in current events and news. I've just been working and training."

"Did you have any contact with Lynne after your interaction online? Or any of the other women who criticized you?"

Nolan stared at Connor like he was mad. "Why would I do that? I hated Lynne online. Now I'm supposed to go and speak to her in real life? I'm not that way. I didn't want to have dealings with any of them. They're scum!"

"What hours do you work here?"

"Seven to four, every day but Sunday. I don't take breaks. I train clients throughout the day. Everyone knows they can find me here."

"What were you doing the night before last?"

"That night, I was at the local combat club."

"What's that?"

"It's a private setup down the road. There was a match on. I was refereeing. I was busy there from five p.m., until things wrapped up at midnight."

"Can you prove it?" Connor asked.

"Sure," Nolan said. "I'll show you that on my phone, but you'll need to take my handcuffs off. Stop treating me like some crazy criminal. There are photos of me at the fight. I took screen shots of all the scores, too."

"We'll check that," Connor said calmly. "I'm going to take your handcuffs off. Then you can show me. Like I said, one wrong move, and we're going to have a different conversation, at the police department.

While he removed Nolan's handcuffs and checked his phone, Cami was already checking it on her own phone. She'd found the fight club online and was looking at the shots from the competition the night before last. Sure enough, Nolan was there, in color, throughout the evening. Breaking up a pair of struggling fighters. Stepping in with his fists raised.

"Here," she said quietly to Connor, showing him.

Undoubtedly, he'd been where he said he was, and she felt a flash of disappointment because that meant he had an alibi for Davina Bright's murder, and had clearly been busy working at the club when Rosanne Jeremy was killed.

But even so, Cami still thought they were on the right track. With all four of these victims having been active on this website and nowhere else, she was sure it was the right place. They'd identified the hunting ground, but had just gotten the wrong hunter.

They needed to look closely again. Perhaps the killer was not an athlete, but someone who hated athletes and athletic prowess. With those parameters in mind, she could search again.

"Alright. You stay out of trouble," Connor threatened, opening the office door. "You're cleared this time, but if you treat the police this way when they come asking questions, you're going to end up in jail again."

Nolan shrugged aggressively, his old attitude surging back.

"Why don't you respect people's privacy?" he snapped, as they walked out of the office.

On the way out, Cami had to suffer yet another round of hisses and whispers and catcalls. But this time, she found, she was able to take the treatment in a more balanced way.

That was because she'd figured out a way to get payback on the chauvinistic and aggressive members of this gym.

She hesitated for only a moment, when they were outside, before pressing the button on the phone that she hoped would make all their lives a lot worse, immediately.

CHAPTER NINETEEN

As she climbed into the car, Cami pressed the button she'd found to set off the internal sprinklers within Fight Club, that activated in case of fire.

She had a feeling that sprinkler system might predate Fight Club, and had been installed when the place was a warehouse, with a need for effective fire control. Of course, there was a chance that they hadn't been maintained and no longer worked. She guessed she'd soon find out.

As Connor pulled away, Cami saw the man who'd grabbed her arm run out of the building, water streaming from his clothes. He was followed by others, looking wet and angry. Their mood didn't seem to improve when they realized they had been forced to flee out into the pouring rain.

"What's their problem?" Connor asked, braking sharply to avoid one of the men, who'd opened the door of his muscle car as they approached, to shelter inside.

"I don't know. Maybe the building sprung a leak, or something?" Cami said innocently.

Connor gave her another glance. "Remember, you can't go acting like a renegade on cases. We have to operate by the book," he said sternly.

But Cami didn't think his heart was in the admonishment. And she personally felt it was only fair that those sexist, insulting men were now drenched to the bone. They deserved a cold shower after their disgusting whispers and comments, not to mention grabbing her. And it was probably the first time in years the place had been properly washed down, she thought, feeling smug.

"So are we going to follow the theory that the killer has a serious problem with athletes, and in particular, with women?" she said to Connor, hoping to distract him from what she'd done with the sprinklers.

"Yes. Let's think that way. Let's theorize that, in his mind, they're a problem." Connor agreed as he eased the car through the rain, heading back to the main road. Cami guessed that after this unsuccessful outing they would return to the FBI offices, unless she could come up with an alternative destination, and suspect.

"What if he's been outspoken about that, either on the forum, or in public? Maybe he's been standing up for what he believes in by speaking out, and has now decided it's not enough and he needs to act on it?"

"There might be a few men on that board who have that attitude, people being what they are," Connor warned. "You need to look for a strong link to the victims if we're going to start hunting in that direction."

Cami made a start as they were driving, by looking for negative comments on the site. And she discovered immediately that Connor was right. Negative comments had often started what became mini wars, and from the way that people picked sides, she could tell there were quite a few men out there who resented the super-fit women and their achievements.

Reading through the comments, she wondered where she could start. Who was the person who potentially had the biggest grudge and motive?

Here was one angry comment. *"All you women who think you're just as good as men, but show me your running times. Show me one of you who can outrun the fastest man. So - waiting. You can't, can you?"*

Cami didn't think that attitude was necessarily going to trigger a man to murder. But there were others.

"I feel that you're setting a bad example as role models. You need to aspire to being sportsmanlike and encouraging. I have never seen so many egos on one site. Girls, be ashamed!"

That was getting closer, Cami thought, but she still couldn't find any particular links between this male critic, and the victims. He picked on everyone who didn't meet his role model criteria and, in fact, he had also praised the sportsmanship of Lynne Horwood on one occasion, she read.

So, she was going to keep looking for someone angrier.

Connor was now stuck in a long traffic jam formed by a crash ahead. He was tapping the wheel in impatience, but Cami was still wrapped in her own world. She needed to look further. What she was finding wasn't enough.

How about this one, she thought suddenly.

"Female athletes should be eradicated! You are all bringing the wrong sets of values to the table. Women need to know their place.

Your hearts are not in sport. Your hearts should be with your families, as homemakers."

Now this was interesting, Cami thought, particularly the reference to hearts. And the victims had all died from a toxin that mimicked a heart attack?

Who was this man, who she now saw had made snide comments in response to all the victims' posts on their achievements? Of course, the comments had immediately escalated into no-holds-barred conflict on both sides.

"You're an oppressive little man with an outdated agenda. Go back to the Dark Ages," Lynne had written angrily. And he'd replied in a more threatening vein. *"Be careful what you say to me. You are only a weak woman, after all, and you wouldn't want to get that heart rate too high. What if something happened?"*

With her own heart quickening, because she thought she was onto something here, Cami looked him up.

His name was Luke Beyers, he was forty years old, and he appeared to be independently wealthy. He ran the "Women Stay Home" movement, she saw. The website preached that women should return to traditional roles as homemakers, and not flaunt themselves, scantily clad, in competitive sports.

"He even has a wall of shame on his site!" she said aloud.

Connor leaned over to look.

"The Women Stay Home movement?" he asked.

"There's Rosanne Jeremy!" The recent victim was pictured on his wall, smiling, wearing a swimsuit and standing on the winner's podium. "He actually has her. He singled her out. And there's another one. There's Davina. And there's Jill."

"You're sure?" Connor asked, as he tapped the brake. The traffic was moving again, but now he was distracted by Cami's discovery.

"Look for yourself," she said, scrolling through the pictures.

"I see her there. And I see Lynne, too. That's four out of four victims, who have been pictured specifically on the site's homepage. That cannot be a coincidence."

Connor tapped the wheel again, but this time he did so thoughtfully, rather than impatiently.

Cami looked at him.

"What are we going to do?" she asked, hoping that she was right, and that Connor was going to act on what she'd found.

"As soon as we're out of the traffic, we need to go and speak to him," Connor decided. "These links to the victims are strong evidence that he singled them out, and some of what he's said in his diatribe against women in sport is a definite threat of violence. While you were scrolling, I read this comment, just one of many. 'If women won't stay home, they must be forced to by whatever means, and must face the consequences of continuing to disobey.'"

"How can anyone say that?" Cami asked incredulously.

"A good site moderator would surely have stepped in," Connor said.

"Exactly. Leaving those kinds of comments up is asking for trouble. But then again, maybe the moderator thought that the activity on the site and the attention it brought him was worth it. I see that every time they had these fights, new members joined. So perhaps they sacrificed good moderation for the sake of better traffic and numbers."

"Sounds fairly typical of human nature," Connor agreed.

Cami felt cold at the thought that what started with words could then have triggered this man, with his strongly held beliefs, to act on them.

"Perhaps he wanted to get real examples to prove how dangerous it was to be involved in sports, and scare other women into staying home," she suggested. "It looks like he's got a massive ego, from his posts. And he gets very angry when people insult him."

Connor was already finding the address on the map.

"Here's another interesting fact," he said. "He lives in the same local area as three of the victims, and equidistant from two of the murder sites."

"That would have made it easy for him to track them," Cami realized, as Connor changed up a gear, speeding along the road.

"Exactly. This man has some tough questions to answer." Connor said. "And hopefully, he's here to do just that."

And here they were, at the headquarters of the Stay at Home movement, ready to confront the opinionated Luke Beyers, and find out if he'd escalated his methods to murder.

"He's got a rally organized for tonight," Cami stage whispered to Connor, as she checked his website again. "I see he's actually holding a demonstration outside the gym where Jill died."

Cami felt shocked by the timing. The fact that he was holding a rally outside the place where a woman had died so tragically was clearly a blatant effort at capitalizing on her death.

She thought of Jill, being murdered, struggling with the killer alone and in fear, and she felt a burning sensation of anger at the thought of this being caused by a man who was now using the deaths to further his own ends.

"I can't believe this," Cami said, shaken by the callousness of it.

Connor nodded. "Let's get in there, and get the facts from this man."

But, as she gazed at the imposing size of the building, and its sleek, glass-clad frontage, and the luxury cars in the lot, Cami had a nasty feeling this wasn't going to be an easy job and that they were up against a substantial and powerful adversary.

As she headed up the marble steps, she felt as if she was heading into war.

CHAPTER TWENTY

As Cami reached the building, clad in its icy glass, she was uneasily aware that this was not so much a humble headquarters, but a gleaming, upscale corporate abode. She and Connor were up against a level of wealth and power she had not expected from a Women Stay Home movement.

Coming here, she'd expected to be received by a few devoted, if misguided individuals, a dedicated group of men with limited social skills, working tirelessly toward their goal of ensuring women stayed home. But instead, she was confronted with a slick and professional set up, with a spacious interior, that looked to be busy and doing a brisk trade.

Looking around, she didn't see any signage or notification for the rally or the movement. The interior seemed to be bare of signage and notices. But it was clear that no expense had been spared in equipping the place.

The place was decked out like a spaceship, with a huge, silver reception console that swept around the lobby in a magnificent curve. About four people were working behind it at different points, busy helping customers. They all looked well-dressed, motivated, and driven.

To Cami's surprise, there were female workers as well as male workers behind this imposing desk. *What happened to the Women Stay Home ethos*, she wondered.

And what, exactly, were all these customers doing here? There looked to be customers coming and going. This situation was becoming more and more complex.

Cami was beginning to think that this business couldn't be focused only on the movement. Surely there must be some other kind of trade going on in the building?

"Can I help you?" a young, attractive blonde receptionist asked, smiling.

"We'd like to see Mr. Beyers," Connor said.

"Do you have an appointment?" the receptionist asked, glancing doubtfully at the two of them. She was wearing a stylish suit and her hair was professionally coiffed.

"We don't. We're from the FBI. It's in connection with an investigation."

The blonde woman's smile disappeared. In fact, she looked a little frightened.

"I - er - I'll have to check his schedule," she said nervously. She leaned forward, as if taking refuge in her computer screen.

And at that moment, a voice spoke from behind Cami and Connor.

"I'm Mr. Beyers. What is this about?"

They both swung around and stared at the man who had spoken. He looked to have just walked in, and must have arrived shortly after them. Perhaps their FBI jackets had attracted his attention and caused him to come over immediately.

At any rate, at least he was here.

Looking at him, Cami saw that he carried an air of authority about him. He was taller than she expected him to be from a glance at his description online, and he had a fuller head of hair also. But she recognized his craggy features and florid cheeks from the blurry ID photo. He was wearing a sharp, well-cut business suit and carrying a shiny leather briefcase.

"Agent Connor, FBI. We're here to see you."

The man's face paled briefly.

"Me?" he asked incredulously.

"We have some questions," Connor said.

Now looking defensive, Beyers drew himself up to his full height. From his expression, Cami had an instinctive feeling that the word 'lawyer' was shortly going to be mentioned.

And sure enough, the next thing he said was, "I need my lawyers here."

Cami's heart sank. She might not be experienced in investigations, but she had enough mileage to know that as soon as lawyers were involved, things got delayed.

They could not afford delays. Anxiety tautened within her. If this man was their killer, they needed to bring him in and book him as soon as possible. And if he wasn't, then they needed to move on and keep looking.

But even so, Cami knew, this was surely a strong suspect. His motive for keeping women at home aligned with the killer's agenda.

Even though she still didn't understand why so many women were employed here.

"That really is your choice," Connor said calmly, but Cami knew that he was losing patience. "But I'd suggest that you answer the questions here and now, because your organization has attracted some scrutiny."

"My legal team is in the building," Beyers said hurriedly. "Give me a moment."

He turned to the blonde. "Open up conference room nine, will you?"

"Sure," she said, getting up from her seat and hurrying down the corridor. Beyers got on his phone meanwhile, and started making calls. Cami realized he was speaking to his PA.

"I need my team, now. Can you ask them to come downstairs to conference room nine? Yes, everyone. All of them." He paused. "I know they're in that other meeting. Tell them to come back to it later, and step next door for a minute."

She sensed that he was building his defenses up in every direction. She had a bet with herself that three or more lawyers would end up being present at this meeting. At least it seemed to be getting organized quickly. That was the only light she sensed at the end of this particular tunnel.

He disconnected with a sigh. Cami thought he looked seriously stressed. His phone started ringing again, but he glanced at it, frowning, and rejected the call.

The blonde rushed back. "The conference room is ready, Mr. Beyers."

"Come this way," the man said.

He led them down a gray tiled corridor and they headed into a conference room with the number nine on the door. Inside was a steel gray table and eight chairs, as well as some state of the art audio-visual equipment and screens. The walls were strangely blank, and Cami noticed yet again how devoid of signage and branding this place was. It was almost like they didn't want anyone to know what really happened here.

As they headed in, three business-suited men arrived. And a woman in a charcoal power suit. She wasn't staying at home, Cami thought.

They all sat down along one side of the table and Beyers took the chair at the head.

That left the other side open to Cami and Connor. They took their seats, and Cami waited for Connor to start the fight with the suspect.

She was sure it was going to be a fight with this suspect. She remained sure while Beyers glanced at his legal team, who all sat up straighter as if preparing themselves for battle.

She was convinced of it when Beyers himself folded his hands and turned to glare at Cami and Connor.

But then, he spoke, and suddenly, she wasn't sure of anything anymore.

"Whatever my brother has done, I'd like you to know, in the presence of my legal team, and without prejudice, that we are no longer involved with him. In fact, we have taken legal action against him," Beyers announced, in tones that were icy with conviction.

CHAPTER TWENTY ONE

"Your brother?" Cami blurted out the words in surprise before she could stop herself. Her entire set of preconceptions had been turned on their head.

For a start, this man wasn't Luke Beyers. Now she understood the small differences that she'd noticed between the photograph and real life.

This was his brother. And from the sound of things, there was conflict between them. There had been problems, and it sounded as if Luke had caused them.

"You'd better give us the background," Connor said calmly. "Starting with your full name, and the nature of the business you run here."

Beyers glanced at his legal team as if confirming it was okay to proceed. Then he drew a deep breath.

"I'm Leon Beyers. My brother, who's two years younger than me, is Luke Beyers." He paused, eyeing his lawyers again. The lawyer closest to him gave an encouraging nod.

"This is my business. It's called Beyers Worklink. It's a setup where you can rent upmarket, fully equipped office space or conference space in any size, for any amount of time."

Cami nodded to herself. Now, the setup and the lack of signage made sense.

"I've got a few different branches. This is our head office and flagship setup. The business is doing well, especially in such circumstances. We're at eighty percent occupancy today, ninety percent from tomorrow. But I will admit, my brother has been causing us huge problems recently. I tried to ignore it for a while, because family loyalty is important to me, but we've recently been forced to take it further."

"Why's that?" Connor asked. Cami thought she could guess the answer, but waited to see what Leon was going to say.

"Luke has always had very strong opinions. He's always been willing to go against society's norms for no real reason," Leon explained. "He's always been prone to believing misinformation and embracing weird causes."

"Such as the current one?" Connor asked. "Women Stay Home?"

Leon sighed. "If you knew how many headaches that idiotic movement has caused me," he grumbled.

His lawyer cleared his throat warningly, and Leon hastily returned to giving factual information. "He's been involved in various movements and causes over the years. The most recent of these, before his current one, was the anti-government movement. He embraced the idea that government and government agencies are inherently corrupt, and that the public is being duped and controlled by them for financial benefit. I mean, really? Of all the flaky, conspiracy theory, pieces of nonsense!"

The lawyer cleared his throat again, and Leon continued. "At any rate, I was trying to get him to stop, and so I decided to help him with setting up his own business. We are lucky enough to have a small trust fund, so neither of us has to work. I like to work, and enjoy the challenge of running a business. But I thought it was important that Luke worked at something that would keep him out of trouble."

"And what was that?"

"He has always liked the idea of being traditional, of living off the land, being off grid. As you can imagine from the causes he's embraced, that ended up becoming a big part of his ethos. He was keen to promote a return to those traditional family values. Home cooking, DIY, carpentry. He wanted to set up a website and blog, with the help of a developer. I thought that was a great idea. I even gave him an office in this building."

Cami raised her eyebrows. *Was that where the building's address on the Women Stay Home website had come from*, she wondered.

"I'm a busy man. I rush between my branches constantly. It was only a couple of weeks ago that I discovered the blog he'd been talking about had never materialized. Instead, Luke had become obsessed with this Women Stay Home movement. He'd started that instead."

"How did you find out?" Cami asked.

He turned to her, looking stressed. "Because the clients who wanted to rent out our offices began complaining that this was the address of a destructive, anti-establishment movement that was promoting disempowerment of women through force. Seriously, if I'd gotten my hands on Luke at that stage, I would have –"

The lawyer touched his elbow and Leon subsided with a scowl.

"That was a surprise to you, then?" Connor confirmed.

Leon nodded. "It was a rude shock. Since then, we've been doing damage control. I told Luke to leave the premises immediately, and we've since been working on getting all the mentions of our address removed from his website and media. However, we haven't had success there. Hence, the legal action."

"And is he resisting that?"

"He's refusing to take my calls, and he's gone underground," Leon said. "I don't know where he is now. He's proving impossible to get hold of. He obviously wants to keep the address of these offices, because it's a very upmarket location and using it gives him credibility. However, I have a court order in the process, and I am just waiting to serve it."

He glanced at the lawyer again.

"I think you've said enough," the lawyer closest to him advised. "I think you have given these agents a good picture of your circumstances. There's clearly no need for them to ask anything further. It's obvious you are not connected with Luke, and that you've cut ties with him and have distanced yourself from his doings completely." The lawyer paused. "While, of course, not having any violent intentions toward your brother."

He'd been one jog of the elbow away from admitting he wanted to beat Luke up, Cami thought. But she could imagine that it would have been shocking when he'd found out what Luke had done, and that it was now tainting his business. He'd clearly done his honest best to control the damage and distance himself. She was sure that Connor would have more questions, though, and he did.

"I have two more questions to ask you," he said.

"What's that?" Now Leon and all the lawyers stared at Connor with a distinct lack of friendliness.

"I need you to tell me if you can account for your whereabouts and movements, either yesterday evening, or else this morning at about ten, or both. While we're here, we might as well make sure your alibi is confirmed," Connor explained.

Leon frowned. "I was busy yesterday evening at a business dinner that went on late. It was held with my managers from the different branches. We were at my office block in the east of town, in the boardroom. It started at seven and finished at about eleven. We had catering and drinks brought in."

"Okay. Your office needs to confirm that, please," Connor said.

Leon glanced at the lawyer at the end of the row, who immediately got on the phone.

"This morning, I was at a furniture factory," he continued. "I've been there the whole morning, picking out items for a new office block we're launching. I'll give you those details, too." Now that he was on firmer footing, he was speaking with more confidence, and Cami found she didn't doubt his version, although she knew Connor would make sure to confirm it. There was no chance that Leon was lying to the FBI or had been colluding with his brother in the murders. However, she did still wonder whether, despite his angry words, he might want to protect his brother.

"Thank you," Connor nodded.

"And your other question?"

"We need to speak to your brother. He's unfortunately a strong suspect in this case."

Cami thought she was right. Leon wasn't comfortable with that. He frowned.

"My brother's always had a few issues, but he's never really done anything that amounts to a crime. He's always been a bit strange, and I'm really not happy with how he's treating me now, but he's never been dangerous," Leon argued.

The lawyers all started to join in the protest, but Leon held up his hand. "I'll handle this," he said.

He turned to Connor.

Connor shook his head. "Unfortunately the character reference of a brother is not sufficient for us to look away from him. We have to speak to him."

"I understand," Leon said. "But I was telling you that because you'll have difficulty finding him."

"You don't know where he is?"

Leon shook his head. "I have no way of getting a hold of him. I've tried everything. I've asked him to come in for a meeting. I've told him he's putting the business at risk. He hasn't responded to my calls or messages. I think he's angry that I kicked him out of the offices, and now he's refusing to communicate."

"He must be in contact with people, though, if he's organizing a rally outside the gym."

Leon nodded. "Yes. Although I don't know if that will go ahead. Trust me, my legal team is going to be there, looking for him, too. I believe, from the past, that he often changes those plans at the last minute."

"And you don't even have an address for him?"

"I have no idea where he is. My lawyers are working on finding him, but I don't know where to start. He's a free spirit. I don't know who his connections are, or even where he lives. The last address I have is a year old."

"Phone number?"

"That I do have. I guess you can track it?"

Connor nodded. "We can try to locate it. Give it to us, please. And I'd appreciate it if you didn't contact or warn him. This is a murder investigation. Every lead must be taken very seriously."

"I understand," Leon said, as he gave Connor a business card with the details of Luke's phone scribbled on the other side. "I really hope you don't find him guilty, despite his misogynistic ways and the fact that when I see him again, I'm going to punch the daylights out of him."

As they walked out of the room, Cami saw that Leon and the lawyers were now embroiled in a very animated discussion. Shouts could be heard. Connor and Cami left them to their arguments, and headed out of the hotel.

"Do you think he was telling the truth about Luke?" Cami asked, as they got into the car.

"He's a businessman. I'm sure he realizes that it would hurt his business even more if he was associated with a known killer. I believe he has distanced himself. But I also believe he might warn Luke. Even if he uses the warning to try and leverage a favor from him in terms of that address being removed," Connor said.

Cami nodded somberly.

All they had was a phone number, and if he was warned or spooked, she was sure this suspect would run.

Time was ticking down.

CHAPTER TWENTY TWO

Cami realized that Connor wasn't even going to waste time going back to the office. As soon as they were in the car, he began making plans to track down their latest suspect.

"I'm going to call the office and ask for a GPS location on this number. Hopefully, that'll be quick. But in the meantime, see what you can do online. We might need more than one way of getting to this man," he said.

Cami agreed. With his inflammatory views and his propensity for threats, Luke Beyers was likely to be very good at keeping low. Cami personally didn't know if she believed that Leon really didn't know where he lived, and she didn't buy his promise that he wouldn't try and get hold of him to warn him.

With any luck, his legal team would advise him not to, she hoped, but there was always the matter of blood running thicker than water. Cami felt sure that was what that loud argument had been about, and if Leon won the argument, then he'd be on the phone in a flash.

She looked at the number scribbled on the back of the card, and keyed it into her phone.

What could she find on it? Was it listed anywhere? Even in a more hidden location?

She found a social media account linked to it, but it looked like a fake account, mostly with posts and comments that were anti-government, anti-corporate, and anti-police.

"It can't be tracked," Connor said, sounding resigned. "The number's not on the network."

She was starting to get a bad feeling about this. Cami had the feeling that Luke Beyers was racing ahead of them and turning back to laugh.

She went back to the website with the chat forum, where he had been so outspoken and critical. The nasty comments were all there, with his IP address, but when she tracked the location it gave her a series of errors. Again, it pointed to a man who was on the move, using different locations and different devices.

What about that website his brother had mentioned? The one he'd started, or pretended to start, blogging about home remedies and recipes?

"I'm not having any luck either," she admitted to Connor. "I'm going to try one last direction here, and see if I can find that site his brother mentioned. Maybe he interacted on that for a while, and forgot to cover his tracks when he switched focus."

She went hunting.

It was pretty easy to find the site, once she had the keywords she needed. Unfortunately, the site was down. All she could track, when she dug, was a big "Out of Service" notice.

"Nope," she said, feeling unbelievably frustrated that she still wasn't making any progress. How was it possible that they were spinning their wheels so badly here?

Ideas went through her head. If Leon really had warned Luke, then had he used the office switchboard? Would it be possible to get into that? How about Leon's personal phone? Could she access that, and would it be helpful? What could she do there?

She had so many ideas, and now needed to prioritize the ones she thought would work the best. Leon's personal phone was probably the quickest starting point. If she could get at least partway into that, it might give her an updated or alternative number. Or show her if he'd just tried to call his brother.

Cami began working, feeling frustrated all over again by the slowness that she was experiencing. Tech wasn't always lightning fast when it came to hacking, and this was one of those times.

Connor sighed. "Seeing we're not getting anywhere, I guess we need to go back to the office. It's easier to work from there," he said.

He started the car, but as he did that, the radio crackled.

"We've got a location on that phone," someone from the FBI office said. "It's just come up on our tracker. The phone's open, and it seems like he's on the move."

Cami glanced at Connor, feeling encouragement flare inside her. They were finally getting somewhere, and it was with the help of the FBI. She was still annoyed that she hadn't been able to get results, but at least they were finally going to get where they needed to be.

"I'm getting the details in, now," the voice said. "It's heading from the city, and looks to be going out of town. I'm going to plot it on a map for you now, and share it. Then you'll see it as it moves."

"We'll head there immediately," Connor said. The map flashed into view on his phone's display screen. "We may need backup, because we're still a few miles away," he said.

"I can get a team out there, but also not immediately," the man on the radio said. "I'll work as fast as I can."

"And we'll do the same," Connor said.

He hit the gas, pulling onto the road, veering into the fast lane. The chase was on, and Cami stared anxiously ahead as Connor wove between the slower moving cars, activating his flashing light, but not his siren.

Connor was gripping the wheel, and although he seemed calm, Cami knew that he was as tense as she was. They were following the flashing dot that represented the phone, as it made its way out of the city and into the suburbs.

Cami felt the excitement building inside her. They were getting close. If a backup team could get there in time, it would help them even more. If this was the last step to finding the killer, then there was no time to waste.

The dot was still moving. They were getting closer. But the dot was traveling fast, and Cami now saw that Luke had reached the highway.

Again, she worried if his brother had warned him. He wasn't driving slowly, because if he was, they would have gained more ground by now. Luke Beyers was speeding, just as they were, and Cami wondered and worried if he was fleeing.

Why would he be running?

Did he know that he'd been identified as a suspect, because he'd been warned? Or worse, did he know that the FBI were coming for him?

"At least his phone's on," she said. If he turned it off now, they would lose him again. She wondered why it was on. Perhaps he was on a call, or using his map app to get where he needed to go. Speed was of the essence here, because if that dot disappeared, then so did their chances of finding him.

Which car was he driving, she wondered suddenly. If she could link a vehicle to his name, that would help them a lot.

Cami went looking, this time using the police database to see if she could get anywhere. She looked up his name, and then searched to see if there was anything listed.

"We're getting close." Connor's voice, sounding excited now, interrupted her focus and Cami glanced up.

Ahead were two slow moving trucks, and beyond was a knot of cars traveling faster. But now they had to wait for the marginally faster truck to overtake the marginally slower one.

"Come on, come on," Connor urged the driver, tapping his hand on the wheel.

And then, glancing down at the screen, he let out a heartfelt curse.

"His phone's gone off. He must have finished a call and turned it off again."

At that same instant, the information flashed up on Cami's screen.

"I've done a search for a vehicle. There's a blue Honda listed in his name. If any of those cars ahead is a blue Honda, that might be his. And we can keep up with him if it is."

With leisurely slowness that made Cami's blood pressure rise, the truck in front of them finally pulled into the slow lane again.

Connor flattened his foot, accelerating as fast as he could to the group of cars ahead.

"I see two blue cars," Cami said, leaning forward and feeling excited. "And one's a Honda. The one on the left. If you can get closer, I'll tell you if the number plate matches." She waited a beat, and then nodded. "It's the same one. It's him!"

"That's our man, for sure," Connor said.

But even as he sped toward the blue Honda, the car swerved violently, nearly causing a crash as it veered into the other lane, heading desperately for a nearby exit.

Luke knew he was being chased. And he was doing his utmost to get away.

CHAPTER TWENTY THREE

Cami felt certain now that the irrational, elusive Luke Beyers was behind these killings. His aggressive and threatening behavior proved it. His deluded mindset proved it. And now, the fact that he was panicking when he'd seen the lights of a law enforcement car behind him, proved it most of all.

Connor swore, wrenching the wheel to the right, and Cami ducked instinctively in her seat as the car veered across the lanes, tires wailing.

She didn't care about the danger. All that mattered was that they caught him. If they overshot this exit, then she felt sure that he would make a clean getaway, and would vanish into anonymity - at least, for long enough to commit further kills.

"He turned left," Cami hissed through clenched teeth, as the car rocked and fishtailed on the road. A horn blared, seemingly on top of them, as a semi roared past, its chrome gleaming, its wheels hissing on the wet road.

Without any phone GPS to track, or any likelihood of one in the future, they could rely only on keeping sight of the car in the wet and misty conditions.

"Left. Got you."

Connor swerved to the left, behind another car. They were going so fast that the world seemed to be moving in slow motion, everything at once sharply focused, and yet strangely confused.

Cami could see the glow of red lights ahead of them, and the shape of the car they were chasing. Connor's foot was hard on the gas pedal, and their car was gaining on the other vehicle, but not by enough.

"We're going to lose him," she said, her voice tight. Her hands were clenched in her lap.

"We've still got some tricks up our sleeve." Connor got on the radio again.

"Backup urgently required! Backup required on the intersection of Main and Vine, heading north."

Then, he activated the siren and swerved into the emergency lane.

The car in front of them, a couple of hundred yards ahead on the narrow road, was weaving left and right, and as Connor sped along with his siren blaring, Luke did another of the death-defying turns, taking the car to the left.

Again, Connor had to hit the brakes, burning rubber as he half-sped, half-skidded across the road, to take the same side street as Luke had just darted down. He was driving like a desperate man. This was a last ditch attempt at escape. He was now going to do whatever he could to lose the cops. And they somehow needed to keep up, until backup arrived, or until they got close enough to force him off the road.

Cami tried to persuade herself that they were almost there, but in reality, the situation was very different. Luke was taking insane risks, veering all over the road, making death-defying turns with no warning.

Following behind, Connor had way more responsibility. For a start, it actually mattered to the FBI that they kept other cars on the road safe, Cami knew. He couldn't do what Luke was doing. Without making sure he wasn't endangering anyone else, he couldn't mimic these mad maneuvers. She could see the state of alertness he was in, how his hands were tense on the wheel, his head turning from side to side, assessing and updating the traffic situation as he tried to follow the tortuous rollercoaster ride that Luke was leading them on.

Up ahead, the road widened, and Luke pulled into the outside lane, and sped down the stretch, then skidded left almost without braking at all. Tires screamed, and the car swerved sideways, with Connor's car just behind.

They were on the straight, and Luke was now speeding up. Connor did the same, staying as close as he could. He was working the wheel like a pro. Cami could see the concentration in his face. He was taking chances, but they were the best chances they had.

Luke's tires squealed as he ducked into a side road and took a left, then another left.

Connor followed, and Cami's stomach fell away as they roared around the bend.

In front of them, Luke's car was weaving into the oncoming lane, with horns blaring as angry drivers evaded the reckless fugitive, but Connor had to brake. Cami could see that he was staying close, but he had to be careful. On this stretch, there were now cars in front and behind them. These roads were narrow. Way too narrow for the type of driving this man was doing. What if he crashed? Cami's stomach constricted at the thought that someone innocent, even a child or an animal, might pay the price.

"The sooner we get to him, the sooner we can stop this," Connor said through a clenched jaw.

Cami realized that on this road, they at least had a chance. There were no turnoffs for a while. The road ran, narrow and winding, into a series of hills. They'd left the other traffic behind at last, and if they could stay close enough they might get to him. Connor's car was more powerful than Luke's, and Cami now saw that, although desperate and reckless, Luke's lead had been achieved more through luck than skill. Now that they were on a narrow and winding road, the lack of skill was starting to show, although the danger was ramping up.

With a sick feeling in her stomach, Cami feared there could only be one end to this reckless flight.

Connor's car was about to overtake Luke's when it happened.

She saw the taillights blaze ahead of them as they passed a turnoff, and realized that Luke was now in a skid he couldn't control. He'd taken it past its limits, had tried to turn, and ended up losing control of the car completely.

"Hang on tight," Connor warned.

They were going way too fast. She could see it, in her mind's eye, too clearly. Luke had put his brakes on, and he'd skidded. His car had spun out of control and he'd left the road completely. His car spun onto the grassy sidewalk, and veered across the road.

Connor yanked the wheel to the right and turned into the inside lane, but he was going too fast.

The trees flashed past them, and she saw Luke's car was heading straight across the road, head on, in the path of their car.

It seemed to happen in slow motion as Connor slammed on the brakes. Tires shrieked and the air was filled with the smell of burning rubber. In the next moment, Connor jerked the wheel to the left, and their car began to spin out of control.

Cami had the sensation of flying. She saw the road rushing past. She had time to feel a strange calmness as she thought of Ethan, knowing he'd embraced risk like this every day of his working life with the FBI, and he'd done so with courage and resolve. It was the way he had lived his life. He'd known that his job was dangerous, and he'd done it anyway.

As they began to spin, she closed her eyes.

And then, to her amazement, Connor steered out of the skid. The tires regained their grip on the wet road. The car's headlong pace slowed, but this time, in a controlled way. Their speed bled away, leaving only the frenzied pace of Cami's heart.

They stopped, in a calm and controlled manner, on the side of the road. Connor immediately activated his emergency lights, just as calmly as if he'd pulled over to check a tire.

They were still alive. The car was undamaged. They hadn't hurt anyone in this crazy chase that had so nearly ended in fatality.

But, even while Cami was gathering her shocked thoughts and processing the fact she was alive and unhurt, Connor was wrenching the door open, staring back at where Luke's car had disappeared.

"We've got a suspect to catch," he muttered, and then he was gone, racing down the road.

Cami only had time to utter a swear word as heartfelt as the one Connor had said earlier.

And then, she was racing after him, dreading what they might find when they reached the place where their suspect had crashed.

CHAPTER TWENTY FOUR

Cami pounded along the road, flinching as a passing car drove through a puddle, sending a spray of water arcing over her. Luke Beyers had driven off the road. She'd seen his car spin and slide and then veer over the embankment.

He might be seriously hurt, or even killed. But if he was unhurt and alive, then this headlong flight that had endangered so many lives along the way, was absolute proof of guilt.

Luke had been fleeing the police, and he had something to hide.

There were the skid marks ahead, deep, dark gouges in the soft green grass.

And there was the embankment he'd driven down. She held her breath, scared of the sight as she rushed up behind Connor.

In the distance, she could hear the faint shrill of sirens approaching, and guessed this would be police backup arriving, since nobody had yet had time to call emergency services.

The embankment was steep, but it was guarded by a row of thick, bristly bushes, and beyond that, the slope leveled out.

Cami caught her breath as she saw that Luke's car had been effectively trapped by the bushes. It was securely wedged, hood down, with steam gently hissing from the engine. The car looked remarkably undamaged, she saw in surprise. There were a few dents and buckles, but overall, it was by no means the twisted wreck she'd expected to see. Those bushes had done a good job of acting like a natural safety net.

Inside, she now saw Luke was struggling with the driver's door, which seemed to have been misaligned by the impact. As she watched, the door burst open, and Luke half scrambled and half fell out.

Within a moment, Connor was sliding down the embankment himself, slipping on the steep grass. No way was he going to allow the suspect to escape at this late stage, Cami saw, with a flash of pride.

He had the handcuffs ready in his hand, and he had them around Luke's wrist before the disoriented man had time to do so much as get his balance.

"You're not going anywhere," Connor growled.

"Let go of me!" she heard Luke respond, sounding angry. His voice was very similar to Leon's, she thought.

"You're getting checked over by the medics, and then your next stop is the police department. I don't know what the hell that was about, but you have a lot of answers to give us. You're under arrest, Luke Beyers!" Connor said, breathless with the effort of the sprint, and the tension of that rollercoaster ride pursuit.

"You can't do that," Luke protested as he struggled for balance. "I haven't done anything wrong."

"I disagree. Do you want a list?"

Cami could see that Connor was going to have a tough job hauling this unwilling suspect up the hill, but luckily at that stage, the sirens got louder and the backup car appeared, powering at speed around the bend.

Cami waved it down, and the unmarked vehicle pulled to a stop and the driver switched off its light and siren.

Then, two FBI agents climbed out.

Cami didn't know who they were and hadn't seen them before, but quickly directed them to the slope where Connor had captured the suspect.

"He's down here," she said. "I think he'll need some help getting this man up to the road again."

While one FBI agent placed traffic cones by the side of the road, the other scrambled down and grabbed Luke's other arm. Now, bracketed between two fit, strong agents, there was no more chance for Luke to resist. She heard his angry cries of complaint as the two agents half-dragged him up to the level of the road.

"You've ruined my car!"

"You ruined it yourself, as we'll explain in detail when we charge you with reckless driving," Connor warned.

"Why did you chase me? Any normal innocent person would have panicked to see you chasing me that way!"

"Any normal person would not have assumed the police were after them the minute they saw a light behind them. Were you warned? You switched your phone off, we saw."

Luke glanced down at the phone, looking momentarily even guiltier than he already did.

"I didn't want to be bothered with it. It's a personal device."

"We're going to need you to open that phone, to check where you have been interacting. And with whom."

More sirens indicated that the paramedics were now arriving. Connor turned to greet them as the two men climbed out of the response car and hurried over.

"I'm fine!" Luke protested. "There's nothing wrong with me. I don't need paramedic attention. I'm not hurt in any way. I had my seatbelt on."

But already the paramedics were checking him out, asking him detailed questions, and asking him to move his limbs to ensure there were no breaks or fractures.

Once they had given him the all clear, Connor took Luke by the arm and escorted him to the unmarked car. Cami got in the front, and they headed to the nearest police station.

Cami still felt as if she was shaking all over from the high speed chase. She wasn't sure how Connor was able to act so calmly. How had he been able to recover his cool so quickly, after they had literally been a hair's breadth away from a serious crash?

She knew that moment when the car had begun to slide, that panicked clench of her stomach as she realized they'd lost control, would haunt her nightmares for a long time to come. But at least the terrifying drive had a good outcome, and now the suspect in the back would have to give answers.

They arrived at the police station and Connor unloaded Luke, took him in, and processed him quickly, before hustling him through to the interview room.

"Now, we are going to get what we need from you," Connor said in satisfied tones, as he stared at Luke.

It was interesting to see the difference between the brothers, Cami thought, as she looked at the man opposite them. The physical resemblance was clear, but Luke had shifty eyes. His gaze slid away from Connor. He had a scrape on his cheek from the car crash, and his hair was wilder than his brother's. His eyes were wilder too. There was something in his expression that Cami thought showed he was a loose cannon.

His demeanor showed it too, as he half-stood in his chair, saying, "These cuffs are painful! They are digging into my wrists! Take them off. Don't I have rights?"

Connor shrugged, looking totally unsympathetic.

"You forfeited your rights when you put other people's right to safety at risk. But that's not what I want to talk about now. I want to

109

talk about your organization, Women Stay Home, and the extreme lengths you might have gone to in order to prove your point."

Now, Luke looked appalled.

"What are you implying?" he asked.

"I am implying that you deliberately murdered four of the women that you fought with on the sports performance forum website. And that you singled them out on your website, with photos of them on your home page. They were clearly a problem to you. A threat."

"But - but, wait -" Luke stammered out. "That's not my site!"

"You say you don't head the Women Stay Home movement?" Connor's voice was sharp and Cami knew he was not going to accept a lie.

"I do. I do head it."

"You knew those victims. You must have been following them on the forum."

"Of course I was," Luke said slowly, looking a little sick. "I wanted to see what they were up to. To see if they had learned their lesson. I wanted to see if they would start staying home where they belonged."

Cami thought he looked confused. He was blurting the words out as if he didn't even correctly understand what he was saying. He was not a logical person, that she saw immediately.

"Each of the four women was murdered within the past few days," Connor continued implacably. "And you have been difficult to find. No current address, your phone turned off much of the time. You have clearly been trying to keep below the radar while you take action."

"This is crazy!" Luke exclaimed. "Why should I want to kill anyone? I'm a pacifist!"

"A pacifist who says women should be forced to stay home?"

"It's a free country. I can say what I want. I can put up a website. It's my right."

"Right. So now that you've admitted you were willing to force these women to stay home, let's talk about your alibi," Connor said, giving Luke a piercing look.

"Alibi?"

"The times and dates of the murders. We need to find out if your time is accounted for."

Now, Luke looked panicked.

"Wait a minute. You can't do this to me. My time? What if I - I haven't been around anyone?"

"Then it will make the case against you stronger. At the moment, that case is already strong. But there's never any harm in building up the proof."

"I've been alone the past few days," Luke muttered. "I - I was staying at a friend's house while he's been out of state. I'm trying to avoid my brother because he's victimizing me. I haven't been taking any of his calls. I don't know how I can account for my time."

"Yesterday morning? Any meetings, any interaction with anyone?"

"No. I didn't speak to anyone yesterday. I was busy writing a blog post but it wasn't ready to go live."

"How about the previous day, in the evening?"

"Look, I was at home. Working on my blog and planning the rally. The rally takes a lot of planning. We often have to change venues."

"Do you go on the dark web often? Order anything from there recently?"

"I don't know what you mean!"

"I'm going to need to take a look at your messages, your maps app, and your communication over the past few days. Open your phone," Connor demanded, taking Luke's phone out of the tray where it had been placed, and handing it to him.

Luke stared at it. Then he stared at Connor and shrugged. "I can't open it," he said.

"If you don't open it, then our IT expert will open it for you." He glanced at Cami. "So you might as well open it."

Now, Luke gave her a pleading glance. "You open it. Go on. I'll tell you the code if you like."

Cami stared at him in surprise. "Why don't you open it?"

Luke looked down. "I can't read that screen without my glasses. It's just a double blur. I'm severely astigmatic and I'm far-sighted. I can't read numbers on a screen at all."

"And where are your glasses?" Connor asked. "You must have glasses?"

Luke shook his head. "I think they must be in the car. They fall off all the time, because they're very heavy. I think they fell off during the crash. So I'll tell you the code. It's 236842. You might need to point the phone at my face as well. Then you can take a look, if you like, but I haven't been using it much. I will admit, my brother called me earlier. I didn't take the call. But then, when I saw you, I panicked anyway."

Cami took the phone. She keyed in the code. She activated face recognition and the screen blinked open.

But, as she began looking through the apps and activities, she felt filled with doubt at what she'd just been told.

Luke Beyers was severely farsighted, so much so that he relied on a pair of badly fitting glasses to see a small screen at all.

Cami was wondering how on earth he'd managed to have a prolonged struggle with each of his victims, before reading the setting on their fitness watches to get their heart rate at death.

Wearing loose, heavy glasses didn't seem like a logical possibility during this scenario.

Something wasn't adding up.

CHAPTER TWENTY FIVE

"So, what do we have on the phone?" Connor's voice interrupted Cami's worried thoughts, and she focused once again on the content of the device. This was important, and she didn't want to be distracted, especially with Luke frowning at her. Even if he was frowning because he couldn't see her face clearly, it was still off putting.

"Do you mind if I step outside?" she asked.

"Let's both go," Connor said.

They got up and walked outside. Connor closed the door of the interview room, and locked it. Then he gestured for Cami to walk down the passage. Here, in the police station's small side office, Cami felt more comfortable being able to check the phone, while not being scrutinized by Luke.

"I'll take a look now," she said, perching on an empty chair. Scrolling through, she began to analyze his recent activity, but she couldn't get the questions and doubt out of her mind.

Maybe Luke was lying about his eyesight, she thought, or just trying to make out like he was a weaker person than he really was.

He might be trying to create the impression that he hadn't been capable of the murders, whereas in reality, he was a tall, broad-shouldered man with a strong build. There was no physical reason why he could not have killed those women. Certainly, the crazed way he'd driven showed he had a big appetite for risk and was not scared to put himself in danger.

But that eyesight?

Eyesight was such an important part of interacting with devices. Cami knew herself how tired her own eyes got after an intensive session on screen, and how some of her classmates at MIT battled with eyesight and needed different glasses for different screen distances.

The fitness watches were a problem. The heart rate display on a fitness watch wasn't big. And if he'd been unable to read the numbers on the keypad to access his phone, he would have been unable to read the numbers on the heart rate monitor. And those scrawled numbers had been accurate. Without a doubt, they matched the readings.

Unless he'd somehow managed to keep his glasses on, and unbroken, during four separate physical fights, in which all the women had lost items of clothing, and received cuts and scrapes. Had he done that?

She hoped that somehow, the interaction on his phone would incriminate him despite her misgivings.

"I'm going through the messages first," she said to Connor. "He's been communicating with several people over the past few days. But there's nothing that seems to point specifically to these women. He's been messaging a few of his connections about the rally. He's received texts from his brother but he hasn't replied. He must have a laptop or some other device because there are no emails on this phone, and no recent calls, although he could have deleted his call record."

"So we need to look further," Connor said. "He probably has a laptop at home that we can't access at this point," Connor said. "He could have been doing all the communicating from there. We can seize it if we need to."

Cami nodded. She had been thinking much the same.

"What about the maps app? I want you to go through his maps app now," Connor said. "See if he's visited any of the locations of his victims. And, I want you to check out his web history as well. I want to know what he's been researching."

"He's been driving around several fitness venues, and several gyms. Those are listed in his map history. But that doesn't mean he would always have used the map. If he was clever and thought ahead, he wouldn't have done that."

She was frustrated that the evidence they were getting seemed to be almost enough, but not quite. If Luke was highly intelligent then he might have done all this purposely to cover his tracks. But Cami was now wondering how intelligent he was. Certainly, he was cunning. He was devious. But logical? A planner? She hadn't seen so much of that coming to the fore, not even in his rally organization. It seemed to be haphazard.

He also didn't seem to have an in depth knowledge of IT. And yet, he'd had a website for the Women Stay Home movement.

So the question Cami was now asking herself was this. Had he created that website? Or had he gotten someone else to do it, a developer, someone who had more IT knowledge than he did.

And that brought another question to mind. It was based on something Luke had said.

114

"Connor, he said when we were interviewing him that the Women Stay Home site wasn't his," Cami said.

"Yes. But that was clearly a lie."

"Maybe it wasn't a lie," Cami said, now considering exactly what Luke might have meant. She had to admit that he hadn't been in circumstances that would encourage logical thought. He'd just been in a car crash, and then gotten arrested. That was going to be enough to rattle even a logical person.

If Luke wasn't logical to start with, he might have just reflexively responded to that question without then explaining exactly what he meant.

"It must have been a lie, surely?" Connor frowned. "Being his movement?"

"The movement was his, but the site wasn't. I don't think he explained it properly, or even realized the importance of what he was saying." Now, Cami thought she was getting somewhere with this reasoning. "Connor, I'd like to go back in and ask him a few more questions. I think it could get us somewhere."

"Then let's do it," Connor said. "If you're not finding any clear evidence from the phone, we need to push this one way or the other. Either we must find him guilty some other way, or else clear him."

Cami didn't like the thought of that, because if he was cleared, they would have to start the search again. But now, she had the tiny ghost of an idea as to where they could look next.

She got up and walked back to the interview room, together with Connor. Luke was sitting at the desk, his head bowed, fidgeting with his handcuffs. He looked up when Cami walked in and, again, she noted that he seemed confused, upset, and disoriented. He didn't look sharp, organized or together. Not at all.

"I wanted to clarify something with you," she said.

"Sure," he said, his voice flat, as if he'd given up on any hope of being released, or things working out for him.

"Your website. You own it, right?"

"Yes. I own it."

"But did you design it?"

"Well, I mean, I came up with the ideas, the themes. I decided we needed a blue logo because it's a strong masculine color. Like a man was telling a woman to stay home."

Cami continued, trying to be patient with the disorganized Luke, whose ideas about where women should stay she quite frankly despised.

"Who built the site? Was that you?"

"Oh, no. Someone did that for me. Someone helps me with it, and I pay to get it done."

Now it was time for the most important question of all, the one that Cami now realized she'd missed earlier.

"The photos on the site. Who chose them? Did you choose them?"

"I didn't choose the photos on that homepage. They were chosen by the site designer, the guy who builds and updates the site. He said he'd pick the ones that would work the best."

Now, Cami exchanged a glance with Connor and saw his eyebrows raise as he realized the implications of this. Cami knew this was a major break in the case.

"So you didn't choose those photos on the site. You didn't even know what the photos were when they were chosen?"

The four victims had been on that site's homepage, and he hadn't put them there. That meant someone else had. Cami felt suddenly breathless.

"No. I'd seen them on the website, of course, but I didn't even know they were going to be used on my site until they were all published."

"And they're all from the fitness forum? All those photos?"

"Yes, they are. There are hundreds on there. He had many to choose from."

"Is that developer on the chat forum site too?" He must be, Cami thought, if Luke hadn't known which photos were going to be published

"Yes, he is. I mean, I haven't seen him interact much, but he must be. We private messaged a while ago."

"So he supported your ideas?"

"Oh, yes, he said he was fully behind them. When I told him my ideas, he approached me and asked me if I'd be interested in having a website, and that if I ever wanted one, he could design it." Luke stopped himself, as if wondering whether he was talking too much. "What I'm trying to say is that we met on that site. On that fitness forum. And then, he helped me with my site."

Now for the most important question of all. The one that she now believed would lead them to the identity of the real killer.

"Do you know his name?" Cami asked.

CHAPTER TWENTY SIX

"His name?" Cami saw Luke frown as he considered her important question. She felt as if everything hinged on the answer.

"You know, I only know him by his site's username," Luke said with a surprised laugh.

"And what's that?" Connor pressed impatiently.

"His username is 'Jon.'"

"That's it?"

"Yes. Just 'Jon.' He designs a good website, though, I must say. He said he'd give me the best site ever, and I think he did just that."

Luke stared at Cami, as if now finally wondering why she was pursuing this line of questioning.

Cami was now convinced that the lurker on the fitness forum, and the site developer of Women Stay Home, was the killer. He was lurking in the fitness community and the fitness website. He knew about the achievements of these fitness enthusiasts, and could have tracked the victims by their activity on the site. They were all well-known individuals, they all posted personal photos, they all talked about their local gyms, and none of them had interacted anonymously on the site. Plus, the killer that she now suspected to be Jon, clearly did have sufficient IT knowledge to build a website. That would have allowed him to use IT if he had needed to, to do any necessary tracking of his victims.

And if he was a web designer, then he would have found it easy to go onto the dark web and obtain the poison he needed to kill.

With the scope of what she now suspected, Cami could hardly wait to get back to her own computer and see what she could find.

"You've been helpful," Connor said to Luke, who was now looking bewildered and somewhat confused. "But you must have some idea of who he is, surely? You must have a good guess?"

"Not really. I mean, I know he looks at all the women's posts the same way I do. With disapproval. He feels that what's happening is wrong."

"Can you tell us anything about him?" Cami asked.

"I really don't know anything more than I've told you."

"How did you pay him?" Cami asked.

"Oh, yeah. I paid him with bitcoin. I had some I bought a while back, when the price was lower. I thought it was a good investment. I liked thinking that I could make more money while sitting in a chair."

"So, he didn't ask for any other way of being paid?"

"No. We discussed it, but eventually he said it was fine to pay him with bitcoin. He charged quite a lot, but he was going to do much more for me. I had a lot of ideas, and he was going to help me expand the site around those. He's a real professional."

"And what did you talk about? Did you say anything personal to him, anything that might help us find him?"

"Well, of course I shared all my personal views, which he said he agreed with. But that was as far as it went." Now, Luke frowned. "You don't think he could be involved in these - these killings, somehow?"

"That's what we're going to find out," Cami said.

She left the interview room feeling deeply thoughtful. She was totally convinced that this was their man. But now, they needed to find him, and Cami knew it wouldn't be an easy task.

As soon as she was back with her laptop, she logged into the forum and took a look for Jon.

Sure enough, he was almost invisible in his presence there. All there was of him was an empty avatar with no information attached to it at all. She couldn't get deep enough to see when or how he'd first logged in. He'd clearly been on the site for one purpose only, which was to single out the murder victims.

But while he was doing that, he'd gotten into a chat with Luke, and being in contact with Luke had led to the opportunity of building the website. So if he'd opened up at all, it would have been to Luke, because Luke had brought him business and they clearly thought along similar lines.

She had Luke's phone here, and from that, Cami knew, she could log into the fitness forum under Luke's identity.

"I'm going to go in again, this time as Luke," she told Connor.

"What, to read those private messages?" he asked. "You can do that if you go in with his login details, can't you?"

"Exactly," Cami said. "It sounded as if they chatted and interacted a lot. Maybe he let something slip. We've seen that Luke is not a logical person and I think he would have completely forgotten if Jon had told him any personal information. If we go back into the message thread between these two men, we can see for ourselves."

"I like that line of thought," Connor said.

Now feeling eager, as if she was onto a solid lead here, Cami took Luke's phone and logged into the website. It was easy to do. The password was filled in automatically on the device, and again, Cami knew, this pointed to a basic level of IT and security know-how.

Now, she was in the forum as Luke.

Immediately, hordes of notifications pinged up, directing Cami to numerous threads where fights were in progress and people were getting mad at Luke, with his ridiculously outdated ideas and belittling attitude. Outraged comments bombarded her, left, right, and center.

But she didn't have time for those. Nice as it would be to go into each one and apologize unreservedly using Luke's name, what she needed to do now was look for the private message thread with Jon.

Here it was. She found it after a short search.

Cami saw straight away that there were reams of long conversations - from Luke's side, anyway. Jon hadn't said as much. Luke had been the talker and the sharer in this partnership.

"I just can't bear that overly ripped look in a female. I mean, it's hideous. Not what the female form is about," Luke had complained.

"I hear you," Jon had sympathized.

"So ugly! Where's the appeal?"

"There is no appeal."

In another message, Luke had complained, *"Women should not need to be so desperate to get attention that they have to shove their entire bodies away from their natural beauty to achieve it. It's not attractive, it's demeaning, and it's not feminine. But I don't see many people getting that."*

"I agree," Jon had said. *"It's a bad trend."*

"I'm so glad I'm not the only one who thinks like this," Luke had gushed. *"Sometimes I think I'm the only one who sees what's really happening here."*

"I see it too. I always have. I've been angry about this for years," Jon had shared, which made Cami's eyes widen, because finally there was some insight into his character and history.

"This site is a very angry place," Luke had said. *"It's not a happy place at all. The people here are angry and bitter. That's what happens when you don't stay home."*

She'd hoped Jon might then reveal more personal details but he hadn't.

119

Scrolling back past this lengthy diatribe, Cami tried to look for anything that might have encouraged Jon to spit out some of his personal info.

There were more complaints about the female form, a lot of them. There was a commiseration after a few of the athletes had attacked Luke online.

And there, for the first time, she saw some website-based conversation.

"How's the site going? Need anything more done?"

"Yes, soon. I have big plans."

"Great, let me know when you are ready. I'll do them same day."

"I'm working on a new specialist site. I've got some good ideas for it. You know, a site for stay at home moms. I think it could be a winner."

"That sounds great. I'll be ready to go ahead when you are."

Cami decided it might be quicker to search through the direct messages for any mention of 'website' just to check if anything had been let slip when business was discussed. Otherwise, she could spend hours scrolling through these meaningless conversational snippets.

She remembered that Luke had said they'd discussed payment. If she was lucky, then perhaps Jon had given alternative payment instructions and then they'd decided on bitcoin.

When she had that up and running, she then leapfrogged back, bypassing the endless criticism of sporty women, and focusing on the chat about the site itself.

Here was something about payment. Nope, that was just confirming the price for an update. She needed to go back further, to see if anything else had been discussed.

Here was the very first mention of payment, and Cami's heart quickened as she read it. Finally, they had found where this killer had made a mistake.

"I've got something here," she told Connor excitedly.

CHAPTER TWENTY SEVEN

It was time for the skull mask at last.

The killer felt a mix of satisfaction and excitement as he reached for the mask and placed it over his head. This mask covered the whole head, turning his face into a featureless, grinning monster, with white cheekbones and bared teeth.

He was ready for the final kill, the most important one yet. This time the circle was completed. He was back where he started, his mission almost accomplished.

Staring at the house on the hill, he felt his hatred surge anew. This was the place where the torture had happened. This was the place where, daily, he'd been brutally dominated by the man who had tried to control him every minute of the day and night, and who'd tried to change him into an image of who he wanted to be.

"You were no father," the killer spat, his breath hot under the mask as he strode effortlessly to the front door.

He felt the anger surge as he thought of the way he'd been treated, the way that domineering man had stripped him of his childhood and had tried to destroy his very soul. In his mind's eye, he could see a younger version of himself, a boy still, trying to please the man who ruled their house.

The killer had been frightened, and alone, and he'd done what he had to, to survive. Now, he was desperate to get this done. He wanted the final closure. He wanted closure, once and for all.

He wanted to be free.

But even now, those dreadful words scorched inside of him as he remembered them.

"You're weak! You're puny! You were never good enough!"

How could anyone have grown up to be normal and happy when there was a brutal, controlling monster in power?

He could feel the fury rising inside him again. It had been so long building, and now it seemed that it couldn't hold back any longer.

He hated his father for what he'd done, but the killer also hated himself for not having had the guts, the strength, to stand up to the abuse. Yes, he was to blame as well, there was no denying it. There had been more than one culprit in this small house, which stood alone among fields, in a quiet country area a few minutes out of town.

He reached the house. He looked up at it, and there was a sense of homecoming, of a destination reached. A sense of triumph.

"I'm here," he said. "And I'm going to finish it."

He reached the door, and paused. He was ready. He'd waited a long time for this moment. He was about to make his last kill. A kill that would give him the freedom that he so richly deserved.

He reached for the door handle.

He was going to avenge his childhood, and he was going to set himself free. It was time to finally rid himself of all the pain, the hurt, and the years of abuse that had scarred him so cruelly. It only remained to be seen how well he would do it. But of course, he'd already had a lot of practice in that regard.

The door opened easily under the killer's touch. And then he was in the hall. He heard the ticking of the clock in the hall. The refrigerator humming.

Reaching down, he felt the syringe, a reassuring shape in his pocket. He couldn't wait to use it.

In the hallway, he glanced at the framed photo on the wall, feeling his mouth twist into a sneer.

The photo was of his father. A big man with an arrogant, cruel face. A man who'd never achieved the fitness he'd wanted to attain for himself. No, despite being the worst kind of bully, his father had always been flabby, out of shape, more focused on pushing others past their limits than he was in testing his own.

The killer remembered the man in the photo shouting at him, shouting at him every day.

"You're pathetic! You're worthless! You'll never be anything but a runt! A weakling! You're a waste of space! You're a waste of my time! I could crush you with my hand!"

"But you never will," the killer told the framed photo, his voice a harsh whisper. "Because you're dead."

His father had died two years ago, ironically, from a real heart attack, and the killer had thought his death would bring peace to his soul. It hadn't worked that way, though, because he'd felt his hatred and resentment grow even stronger.

There was one person that he now realized was even more to blame than his father. And that was his younger sister.

Tammy had always tried harder. She'd always been the first to buckle under his father's pressure. She'd been the little "yes" girl of the partnership, who had always complied and always tried. Tammy had been the reason he'd been bullied so much.

He didn't care that she'd also suffered, and that many times, he'd heard her crying herself to sleep at night. The point was that she'd made his suffering worse, by trying to escape it herself.

She was the reason that he'd been so brutally pressured, and so cruelly compared to women. His little sister, with her long legs and fit build and her can-do attitude. She was the final enemy and the one he hated the most.

He'd followed Tammy closely. She'd seemed to make a success of her life in a quiet way. He guessed she'd overcome the demons of his father's abuse better than he had. She'd inherited the house - he'd inherited most of the money when his dad had died - and now, she used it as a destination for kids and the elderly to do exercise and physio classes. There were rooms for kids' Pilates, there were jungle gyms outside. There were safe pathways around the house where elderly people could walk, and specially equipped gym rooms to help them with their mobility.

He guessed she felt fulfilled, running such a place, but he knew that it was fake and she was a fake.

Her idea of escaping the house was to build a fake house, a place that was only a pale copy of the original, and try to position it as a destination where she could do good. But he knew the truth. She was not a good woman. How could she have any kindness in her heart after what she'd done to him?

The killer walked up the stairs. Colorful posters were pasted along the wall, with flowers and fields and cartoon figures, bouncing along, enjoying their activities. Motivational posters urged the young people, "Use Your Body! Run and Play! A Healthy Life Means Walking!"

At this hour, the house was empty, and there would be more classes in the afternoon. Usually, of course. Not today. Today, there would be no further classes. Nor ever again.

He could hear her footsteps behind the closed door at the top.

He knew that now, at lunch time, Tammy took advantage of the house being empty to do a short workout on her own in one of the gym rooms. That proved to him all over again how fake she was, how she had complied with their father's bad treatment even after his death. There was no reason for her to do this, but she did.

She was still trying to get approval from a dead man, from a father she'd never really had, from a dead bully who'd been the ruin of her life.

Tammy could run, but she could never escape.

A picture of her swam into his mind. She was a pretty, petite, blonde woman with a slim build, and a sadness in her eyes.

No wonder there would be a sadness there after how she'd been treated. Putting an end to her life would probably be a favor to her. All the people she supposedly helped could find somewhere else to go.

He heard Tammy's footsteps, her breathing. He heard the slap of feet on the treadmill, and her humming.

Then he flung open the door. And heard her scream.

CHAPTER TWENTY EIGHT

"Look here," Cami said. Half rising from her chair in the police department's back office, she felt breathless with triumph at having found what she needed.

"Did he give us something?" Connor asked, hurrying over to her, his face taut with expectation.

"He did. Here's the conversation." Cami turned the phone so that Connor could see, too. "They were finalizing the price of the website work. Luke said: I'll pay you tomorrow and then we can go live. Jon said: That sounds great and the site is ready. Luke said: What are your banking details? I'll wire you the money immediately."

"And Jon gave him the details?" Connor said, sounding pleased and incredulous.

"Yes. He gave his banking details. There they are, see?" She turned the phone to him and pointed, feeling grateful that her intensive search had been rewarded. "But then, he changed his mind. He said: Actually, no, rather pay me in bitcoin. Do you have bitcoin available?"

"And the conversation went on from there, I see, into the merits of bitcoin, and they agreed to use that method as a better option," Connor said, reading on. "But in the meantime, we have banking details that Luke clearly forgot all about."

"Yes. He gave the bank name, account number, and account holder's name. J. Pringle. That would link up with the name Jon. I'm sure it's his account. Can you work from that?"

"I can," Connor said. He got on the phone immediately to the office.

"We're looking to trace a person from bank details," he said, quickly reading out the account number and the name. "How soon can you get that?"

"Give me five minutes," the assistant in the office said to Connor. "That bank's usually quite fast."

Five minutes. It felt like the time was endless. Cami fidgeted as she waited, willing the phone to ring, feeling a curdling inside her stomach as she wondered where J. Pringle was now. Was he at home, planning the next kill? Or was he already out, prowling around the gyms, ready to take down another innocent woman and stab a syringe of toxin into her body?

The thought brought a world of worry with it and she could see that Connor, too, felt as if every second was counting.

Eventually, the phone rang, and he grabbed it.

"Yes?" he said. "Yes, go on?" He scrawled down the details, and turned to Cami.

"We've got an address for J. Pringle," he said. "And a full name. We're looking for Jonathan James Pringle. Alias Jon, I guess. He's thirty years old, and he lives about five miles from here."

"Great!" Cami felt ready to go out on the chase, but Connor wasn't done yet.

"Any cell number?" he asked his contact in the office.

"Not on the main database," she heard the regretful reply.

"Look on the other databases. We need a cell number for this man. If he's not home, we need to know where he is, and be able to track him. Scour the records. And if you find a number, set the GPS tracking up immediately, because we'll have to follow it urgently."

"Will do."

They stood up, and Cami shouldered her bag. Connor dropped Luke's phone back in the tray carrying his other personal belongings, and turned to the cop working at a nearby desk.

"We're going out to find a suspect. The man in the interview room, Luke Beyers, can go down to the holding cells for now. I'll call you when we know more. If we find the killer, then Luke won't be facing murder charges, but you can still go ahead with the reckless driving charges."

"Thanks, Connor," the cop said. "I hope you get the right guy, if he's out there."

"So do we," Connor said, with feeling.

He and Cami rushed out and jumped into the car.

Cami felt resolute as Connor powered onto the road. This time, she was sure; they were heading to the correct suspect. This man had handpicked the photos of the victims to be published on the Women Stay Home website.

Cami didn't know if he'd deliberately intended to frame Luke by putting them there, or whether he'd just loved the chance to display those photos somewhere public while remaining anonymous. Either way, though, it was lucky they had looked further, and worked out the link.

Now, would he be at home, Cami wondered. She had a bad feeling inside her that he might be out, seeking another victim. He seemed to be escalating the frequency of his kills and growing greedier.

She turned to her phone and looked up Jonathan James Pringle, to see if she could find out anything about him online. She wanted to know her enemy. Who was he and what did he do in everyday life when he wasn't stalking people and murdering them in brutal ways? What had made him who he was?

But it seemed as if Jonathan James Pringle had lived his life under the radar, as a recluse. Perhaps he had private wealth, she reasoned, because she couldn't find any mention of him on a job site or anywhere else on the web. There were some references to schooling, which she saw had been in Boston, but more than ten years ago. The school's yearbook wasn't available online so she couldn't even see a photo of him. Perhaps there was an official ID photo on the databases the police could access. But elsewhere, nothing.

"He's an invisible man," she told Connor, who was now speeding along the main road. "There's no mention of him online at all." She paused, as her phone updated with another search. "Oh, wait. There's something here."

"What's that?" Connor sounded focused as if he, too, wanted to know his enemy.

"It's an obituary." Cami made a surprised face. "So that can't be him. At any rate, I hope not."

"He's still alive according to the records," Connor said, but now he sounded worried.

"In memoriam, Jonathan James Pringle. Died tragically from a heart attack at age fifty-eight. He is survived by his two children, Jonathan James and Tammy Agnes."

"So that's his father?"

"Must be. He died two years ago. I've got an address for him," Cami said. "His house is out of town, about five miles from here."

"So the father died two years ago?" Connor said thoughtfully.

"I wonder if that caused Jonathan junior to change, and to start having murderous ideas? There must surely have been a reason or a trigger for him to have started doing that, at age thirty?"

"If he is the killer. Remember, we don't know yet," Connor warned, reminding Cami that she couldn't allow herself to get too wedded to her theory without providing corroborating proof.

"If it's him," she acknowledged reluctantly.

At least they would soon know, because they had arrived. But, Cami immediately saw that they were not going to get lucky at Jonathan James Pringle's home address.

The place was locked up. The curtains were drawn. The small house, with a strip of straggly yard between the front door and the road, was very clearly empty. To make sure, Connor walked up and hammered on the door, with Cami waiting anxiously behind him, checking the road, wondering if he might appear at any moment.

Then Connor walked around the house, hammered on the back door, and looked for any windows to peer into. But everything was closed up tight. Looking at the rickety garden gate, Cami saw there was mail sticking out of the mailbox. He was not home.

Connor got on the phone again and switched it onto speaker.

"Any luck with a cellphone number?" he asked.

"We're on it. We've found a cell number registered to Jonathan James Pringle," the man on the other side said. "We're just tracking it now."

"Quickly," Connor said.

He paced up and down the sidewalk, and then, finally, the man on the other side came back on the line.

"We got a track," he said. "You just missed him. It looks like he must have left his place of residence about five minutes ago. And now, he's driving east. And fast."

"Look up his vehicle. If he has a vehicle listed in his name, get an APB out on it. Meanwhile, I need you to link me up to that GPS tracking. We'll follow in the car."

If they could catch up in time, Cami hoped they might stop him before he continued with this deadly killing spree. Now, everything hinged on what would play out in the next few minutes. She felt her pulse accelerate as Connor hit the gas, flattening the pedal as he sped east.

CHAPTER TWENTY NINE

Cami listened to the radio crackling with urgent voices, hoping that more information would come through soon, that would help them reach this killer. A phone GPS was a good lead, but as she knew from experience, it wasn't reliable. Phones could go out of range or be turned off, as the recent chase with Luke Beyers had proven.

A vehicle description would help them a lot. If only they knew where he was heading. East could mean anywhere. There were hundreds of gyms and fitness centers in that direction. He could be driving to an athletics track or a public pool. There was literally no limit to the places he might choose, and the problem was that he'd done his research well. He knew where his victims were going to be.

She guessed he'd spent a lot of time and care staking them out, tracking their movements and habits, without being seen or noticed. If he was driving with purpose, she worried that he was heading somewhere for a kill.

"What's the map showing?" she asked.

She couldn't see the screen. Sometime in the earlier chase, the phone bracket had been tilted sideways. Now, Connor tilted it back again and Cami peered down.

"It seems like he's heading out of town. He's on a main road leading directly out of the city." That was the road Connor was now racing to join.

"Could be going to another town?" Connor suggested. "All we can do is track him, and catch up as soon as we can."

But now, Cami's suspicions were flaring. She wondered if he might have a different destination in mind. She looked back at her phone, and then returned her focus to the screen.

"I think I know where he's headed!" she said. "Look, he's just veered off the main road, and that means he's driving in the direction of his old house, the family home. That's the place where his father used to live."

Her mind boggled as to why. What was he hoping to find in that neighborhood?

Was he going to hunt down an innocent neighbor, someone who'd lived close to the family? Maybe one of the people in the vicinity of his old home was also on that fitness group, and he'd targeted them next.

There were so many possibilities, and Cami worried that no matter which one was the truth, it might end in death and disaster. But he was definitely heading there, and Connor was catching up fast. If they could be fast enough, perhaps they could prevent what she dreaded was about to happen.

As they turned off the main road and onto the smaller, residential streets, they picked up speed. Connor veered onto the street where the Pringles' old house was. It was a long street. There was still a mile or more to cover.

"He's slowing," the voice on the radio came through. "He's stopping outside number forty."

"That's his old house," Cami said, sounding puzzled.

So Jon had gone back home. He was either targeting the new residents of the home, or else, perhaps there was still his own family living there.

His sister, for instance.

Cami felt chilled at the thought. Perhaps this was just a friendly family visit, she told herself. But, with a clench of her stomach, she suspected this wasn't the case.

Connor wasn't slowing. They were powering along, flying past the small homes in their large, treed lots. Cami barely had a chance to take in that this was an attractive area of homesteads, in picturesque grounds, and that the house they were speeding to was on top of a hill.

Connor braked outside.

"That's his car?" he asked. "Must be."

A white SUV was parked at the bottom of the driveway, at an angle, as if the driver had arrived feeling impatient and hadn't bothered to straighten the car. Cami could hear the engine ticking as it cooled.

Connor looked around for a moment, surveying his surroundings, getting a picture of the landscape and the potential threats. The place was isolated, with no neighbors nearby.

The house on the hill didn't have many windows facing the road. But from what Cami could see, the curtains were open, indicating that someone was home. But this man, if he was the killer, would already know that.

Connor powered up the hill and Cami followed, the incline taking it out of her. She felt her legs start to burn.

As she reached the top of the hill, where the pathway curved to the left, she saw with a shock that the front door was standing wide open.

Jon had arrived, and had gone inside. Their killer was here.

Then she froze for a moment, as an unearthly, terrified scream resonated from inside the house. The sound was a woman's voice, without a doubt, and Cami's mind veered immediately back to the sister. Was this Jon's next target? His own sister? Could he have come for Tammy?

She tensed as bangs and crashes came from inside the house. A struggle was in progress. Every second now counted.

Cami rushed into the hall behind Connor. The hall was neat and looked undisturbed. The mat on the floor was straight. Pictures hung squarely on the walls. She saw family photos, a picture of a heavily built man with a grim smile, a much older picture of a blonde woman with two children on her knee. There were also posters, health certificates and signage that told Cami this place was used as some sort of an educational sport facility for schoolchildren and pensioners. Tammy must have taken it over at some stage, either after their father's death, or even before.

The thought flitted through her mind that if Jon hated women who were into fitness, he would have been mad at his sister for starting up a sport school for kids and the elderly.

There had been no fighting here. The hall looked tidy and Cami guessed that meant he'd rushed into the house to find her, rather than ringing the bell for her to come to the door. Perhaps he'd had a door key which he'd kept for years.

The screaming was coming from deeper inside. She listened carefully.

"Upstairs," Connor guessed, powering toward a staircase at the far end of the hall.

He drew his gun and took the stairs two at a time. Cami rushed up behind him. As she raced up, her mind was speeding ahead. What would they find?

The woman's screams sounded terrified, and Cami could also hear the undertones of a male voice, so threatening and angry that it chilled her blood.

A crash caused her to flinch, but Connor didn't even hesitate as he reached the landing and rushed up the second flight.

Connor would be the one to handle a confrontation with the killer - hopefully, at any rate. But Cami might be able to find something else of value in the situation, some other factor, that could be helpful, once they knew more about these deadly circumstances. With that in mind, she didn't follow too closely behind, but instead stayed a few yards back. Maybe it was better this man didn't see both of them immediately. It would mean she'd have the element of surprise or stealth if she needed it.

Connor pounded down a wide corridor. Now, it was clear that the screams were coming from the room two doors down. Pacing behind him with her heart in her throat, she could see what looked like the edge of a treadmill. So this room had gym equipment inside.

Connor didn't hesitate as he powered through the doorway.

"Let her go!" he roared. "FBI. Let her go or I will shoot!"

"Put your gun down, or I will kill her. Drop your weapon or this goes into her neck!" Cami heard the man's reply, sounding full of rage and intent. His voice was strangely muffled. Creeping closer to the doorway, Cami saw his reflection in one of the mirrors on the side walls. His voice was muffled because he was wearing a mask. As he turned his head slightly toward Connor, Cami saw it was a skull mask, a grinning death's head. And death waited in his hand too.

He was holding the syringe, Cami saw, with a thrill of horror as she shrank back. And now it looked as if he and Connor were in a standoff. What could she do?

If this was a gym room, was there another entrance? She needed to find somewhere she could creep around and see what was happening.

Out of habit, she set the program on her phone to search for Bluetooth. Her fingers were shaking. She expected at any moment to hear the sharp crack of a gun, but now she realized that the killer must be using his victim for cover, so that Connor couldn't shoot.

"You don't need to do this," she heard Connor say, sounding calm.

"Struggle, and this goes straight into you," the other man said through gritted teeth, and Cami knew he was talking to the victim he was holding captive.

"Why are you doing this, Jon? Dad was hard on us both!" a woman's voice said, high and shaking. "I also suffered when he got into his moods. He hurt me, too. I'm trying to repair things now. Trying to help kids to enjoy sport and see it as fun, not being forced. To help the elderly and keep them mobile. Why me?" She began coughing and choking.

"Shut up, Tammy!" Jon roared. "You were always his favorite. You made things even worse for me, and now, you're going to pay!"

Cami sneaked into the first room on the right, flattening herself against the wall as she did so, fearing that she'd be noticed or heard, and that he would lose his temper and plunge that syringe into his victim's neck. Once he did that, she knew it would be over. Nothing could prevent the massive heart attack that would follow as the deadly aconite took effect.

The room she was now in was decked out as a small office. There was a desk, three chairs, and a pile of folders. Colorful posters advertising the importance of teamwork and outdoor play were displayed on the walls, with some drawings done by kids, showing them enjoying their sport and having fun.

And there was an adjoining door. Cami's heart lifted.

The door had glass panels, which would allow her to see what was happening, and perhaps she could peek through it without the killer seeing her.

She crouched down and crept close, using the desk as cover, staring through the glass.

The killer had his back to her. He was backed up against a piece of equipment that Cami recognized as a complex weight and exercise machine.

He was using his victim as cover. That was exactly what he was doing. He had his hand wrapped around her throat, which Cami guessed he'd done to stop her talking. He was using her as an effective shield. The bulk of the exercise machine provided yet more cover. No wonder Connor couldn't get a clear shot. Cami saw how the slender blonde was keeping absolutely still, but her hands were shaking violently.

And as for the killer, that syringe was perilously close to her throat. It seemed like he could stab it in at any moment and press the plunger.

Cami thought Connor had seen her. His eyes flickered briefly in her direction before returning to lock gazes with his adversary. If he knew she was there, she guessed he knew she would be trying to help. But she needed to find a way to do it, if Connor was keeping the killer's attention focused.

"You get out," the killer hissed, turning his head to Connor. "Get out of this room. If you don't leave on the count of five, I'm going to kill her anyway."

Cami's eyes widened. This meant she had no time. She'd thought she might have a minute or two, but now it was down to mere seconds.

"There's no need for that. Just let her go, put the syringe down, and step away, and I won't shoot," Connor reasoned.

But the killer was beyond logic. It was as if nothing could penetrate past that grinning mask.

"One," he counted.

Panic flared inside Cami. There had to be something she could do, a way that she could stop or distract him.

She looked down at her phone and saw that it had found something. Various items of gym equipment were coming up on the Bluetooth. This was a smart gym setup, and some of the equipment could be automatically controlled.

"Two!" the killer shouted.

Cami bit her lip. Was there any smart functionality in the machine the killer was backed up against? What was it even called? She wasn't sure which one it was.

"Three!"

"Don't do this, Jon," Connor warned.

T/Mill must be the treadmill. E/Bike was the exercise bike. X/C Mach must be the cross country ski machine. Therefore the only one left was M/Func/Tonal. It had to be that. She pressed the button to access that machine's controls.

"Four!"

"Look, you're going to count to five and it's not going to change things," Connor said, now with an audible note of tension in his voice.

This machine had adjustable, retractable arms, Cami saw. Glancing at the room, she saw the killer was using one of the big, curved steel arms as cover, and also leaning his weight against it.

Move the arms, and it might just surprise him, throw him off balance, or at least delay his deadly agenda.

There was no time left to think about it further. Cami pressed down on the button as the killer shouted "Five!"

CHAPTER THIRTY

Cami held her breath, watching to see if her last-ditch attempt would work as she activated its controls.

Immediately, the machine's arms lowered and retracted in one smooth movement.

With a furious cry, Jon staggered sideways, his support and cover gone. And Connor instantly leaped forward. Cami thought he'd decided that a physical attack gave him a better chance of getting hold of that syringe, especially seeing the killer was still grabbing onto the struggling Tammy.

Now, Connor and Jon were fighting. Jon was yelling in rage, but at least Connor had succeeded in making him free his victim. Tammy rolled out of the way, her face a picture of terror. Connor and Jon were now locked in hand-to-hand combat, wrestling and struggling with each other around the gym machines. This could not be more lethal. In his hand, the killer still held a weapon capable of murdering his adversary instantly.

"Get out of here! Run!" Connor yelled to Tammy, who was sprawled on all fours, coughing and gasping. She immediately did as he said, scrambling to her feet and half-running, half-limping for the door.

But he hadn't let go of that syringe, Cami saw, with a surge of fright. He still had it in his grasp. If Connor wasn't quick enough to get it away from him, then he might still succeed. Anywhere would do. If that needle pierced his skin, if that toxin got into his system, then Connor would die.

The thought that this might happen felt suffocating to Cami. No way could she lose Connor and Ethan, within the space of twenty-four hours. She was not going to let that happen. She had to help.

Cami took a deep breath, focusing on what she needed to do.

And then, she wrenched open the glass-paneled door and she burst through the doorway, leaping for the killer, grabbing his hand with all her strength.

His fingers were scarily strong, and he gave a roar of surprise and rage at this sudden attack. She dug her fingers deep into his wrist, trying to get the syringe to drop, to fall to the floor, but it was as if it was welded into his hand. Even so, she was not letting go. She was not letting him win. Cami hung on for grim death, hoping that by doing this, by keeping him from attacking Connor with his deadly weapon, it would buy her partner some time and space to act.

Now, Cami could feel Jon's muscles bunching and straining beneath her grasp, as he tried to pull her fingers away, but she was not letting go. She couldn't. She felt him sharply twist his arm, and she knew that he was trying to get the needle into her flesh now. The thought made her feel sick.

"No way!" she screamed into his ear, as loudly as she could. He flinched from the sudden sound.

In that moment, Connor took advantage.

He hurled a powerful punch at the killer. His fist crashed into the other man's neck, snapping his head sideways. Finally, Cami felt the killer's hand loosen. She grabbed the syringe and wrenched it free, tossing it aside with a feeling of visceral horror.

"I need to use that!" Jon roared. "Give it to me. It's for my sister. That little bitch had it coming! Daddy's yes girl, all those years. How dare she! How dare she try for him!"

The words were thick with rage, but they were cut short by Connor landing another vicious punch, this time to his solar plexus.

The killer coughed, gasping. Then he flailed, trying to hit back, but he was no match for Connor. He was already hurt and reeling, and now, finally, the tide was turning.

Connor kicked the killer's legs out from under him, and he went down hard, yelling in pain, grabbing at the gym apparatus for balance. And then, Connor launched himself onto him, straddling his body, pinning him down, keeping him still. He dragged the mask off his head and threw it aside.

"You are under arrest," Connor said, sounding breathless but resolute.

The click of the handcuffs signaled to Cami that at last, this fight was over. Their deadly adversary was captured and he would not kill again. Not his sister, nor any other innocent woman.

This danger was past.

And, outside, sirens were wailing as the backup that Connor had requested arrived. A moment later, the team of agents raced up the stairs and burst into the room. She heard one of them outside, speaking to Tammy.

"Are you alright, ma'am? Unhurt? Sit where you are and let the paramedics check you out, I think," he said in concerned tones.

As Connor issued updates and instructions, Cami slumped down onto the exercise bike's seat, feeling as if her legs were too wobbly to take her weight anymore.

"You did well," Connor said in a low voice, standing near her as the other agents dragged the shouting, protesting killer out of the room and began numbering and collecting the pieces of evidence. "You showed exceptional bravery and resourcefulness, and in the circumstances, I never expected you to take on this case with everything you had going on. You proved to me your courage and strength of character. Well done, Cami." He paused. "I'm proud of you. Ethan would have been, too."

"I wish he was here," Cami said, tears flooding her eyes again. They streamed down her cheeks. She couldn't stop them. Didn't want to try.

"It never gets any easier," Connor said. "I wish I could tell you differently. The pain will always be there, especially at that moment when a case is over. All we can do is keep fighting for what he fought for."

Cami nodded, feeling despondent and alone, very different from the way she'd felt at the end of the last case, when Ethan had been there to share the moment with her.

But she wasn't going to give up on Liam Treverton.

His actions might have ended Ethan's life, but she had the voice recording she needed to open Liam's laptop. There was now more than just Jenna's mystery to solve.

She was convinced that this evil ex-agent had been the one who'd sent the gunman in their direction. That he'd recognized Ethan and had wanted to instantly obliterate the threat he represented.

Now, Liam had everything to answer for, and she was going to make sure that he paid the price.

EPILOGUE

Cami stared at the laptop screen as it blinked into life.

She'd ignored everything this morning, as she'd worked to get into Liam Treverton's machine.

She'd skipped her morning class at MIT, calling her professor and saying she would make it up. She hadn't felt ready for studying, hadn't felt ready for anything except this mission. Jacenta had called, but Cami had texted her and said she'd call her back in the afternoon.

Her parents had called, too, which had given her a flash of anxiety, because she didn't know if they knew about her predicament. Were they calling to offer her sympathy because they'd been briefed by someone at the FBI? Or was her dad's number on the caller ID just a coincidence?

It wasn't like her relationship with her parents was good at the best of times. Ever since Jenna's disappearance, Cami's rebellion and resentment toward her father's domineering authority had increased. She still blamed her cop father for not having done enough to find her sister.

Either way, she'd decided that she wasn't in the right headspace to speak to them, and it would be distracting to her as she wrestled with the access to Liam's laptop, so she'd let the number ring through to voicemail.

Exhausted and wrung out as she was, this access was now her only goal.

And finally, she was in. She'd thought at one stage she might feel triumphant when this moment came, but that was before she realized it would be at the cost of Ethan's life, and that this man's evil ran deeper than she'd ever suspected.

Cami hoped that in the next few days, she would learn more about the extent of it, and maybe even unlock the answers surrounding her sister's disappearance.

She had free run of his laptop's functionality, his historic emails stored there, his messages, his hidden archives and records.

Quickly, she ran a program to lock the machine, so he couldn't get in and delete things, or force a permanent shut down.

Now it was hers, to explore and to probe. She was going to find the answers she needed, even if they had been carefully hidden. But something wasn't hidden.

On his laptop, Cami saw that there were controls and screens for his smart home devices. Those were still operational.

She could get into his lighting, his sound system, and to the security alarm in his home.

In fact, that alarm had an info screen, with a messaging function that could bring up notifications. She saw there were historic ones.

"Sensor Four Activated. Sensor One Faulty."

A thought came to Cami. Perhaps she could play with his mind, make him scared, get him worried about what was to come. Paranoid and shaken was what he deserved to be after what he'd done, and that might also make him careless.

He'd taken two of the people she had loved. Jenna and Ethan. And he was going to pay for both. She was going to get the answers and find out who he really was.

She keyed her own message into that security alarm update, not knowing when he might read it, but feeling sure that at some stage, he would. And then, she hoped, when he read these words, he would be afraid.

"I see you, scumbag. I know what you did. And I'm coming for you."

NOW AVAILABLE!

JUST HIDE
(A Cami Lark Mystery—Book 6)

With her tattoos and piercings, MIT tech genius Cami Lark is rebellious and anti-authoritarian—and finds herself in deep trouble when she hacks the FBI. Faced with the choice of prison or aiding the BAU hunt down serial killers, Cami reluctantly partners. A new case, though, has Cami stumped: a string of victims are found dead who look startlingly the same, and it seems a new tech is being used to stalk them. But can Cami crack the code before it's too late?

"A masterpiece of thriller and mystery."
—Books and Movie Reviews, Roberto Mattos (re Once Gone)

JUST HIDE (A Cami Lark FBI Suspense Thriller—Book 6) is the sixth novel in a new series by #1 bestseller and USA Today bestselling author Blake Pierce, whose bestseller Once Gone (a free download) has received over 7,000 five star ratings and reviews.

A page-turning and harrowing crime thriller featuring a brilliant and tortured FBI agent, the CAMI LARK series is a riveting mystery, packed with non-stop action, suspense, twists and turns, revelations, and driven by a breakneck pace that will keep you flipping pages late into the night. Fans of Rachel Caine, Teresa Driscoll and Robert Dugoni are sure to fall in love.

Future books in the series are available.

"An edge of your seat thriller in a new series that keeps you turning pages! ...So many twists, turns and red herrings... I can't wait to see what happens next."
—Reader review (Her Last Wish)

"A strong, complex story about two FBI agents trying to stop a serial killer. If you want an author to capture your attention and have you guessing, yet trying to put the pieces together, Pierce is your author!"
—Reader review (Her Last Wish)

"A typical Blake Pierce twisting, turning, roller coaster ride suspense thriller. Will have you turning the pages to the last sentence of the last chapter!!!"
—Reader review (City of Prey)

"Right from the start we have an unusual protagonist that I haven't seen done in this genre before. The action is nonstop… A very atmospheric novel that will keep you turning pages well into the wee hours."
—Reader review (City of Prey)

"Everything that I look for in a book… a great plot, interesting characters, and grabs your interest right away. The book moves along at a breakneck pace and stays that way until the end. Now on go I to book two!"
—Reader review (Girl, Alone)

"Exciting, heart pounding, edge of your seat book… a must read for mystery and suspense readers!"
—Reader review (Girl, Alone)

Blake Pierce

Blake Pierce is the USA Today bestselling author of the RILEY PAGE mystery series, which includes seventeen books. Blake Pierce is also the author of the MACKENZIE WHITE mystery series, comprising fourteen books; of the AVERY BLACK mystery series, comprising six books; of the KERI LOCKE mystery series, comprising five books; of the MAKING OF RILEY PAIGE mystery series, comprising six books; of the KATE WISE mystery series, comprising seven books; of the CHLOE FINE psychological suspense mystery, comprising six books; of the JESSIE HUNT psychological suspense thriller series, comprising twenty-eight books; of the AU PAIR psychological suspense thriller series, comprising three books; of the ZOE PRIME mystery series, comprising six books; of the ADELE SHARP mystery series, comprising sixteen books, of the EUROPEAN VOYAGE cozy mystery series, comprising six books; of the LAURA FROST FBI suspense thriller, comprising eleven books; of the ELLA DARK FBI suspense thriller, comprising fourteen books (and counting); of the A YEAR IN EUROPE cozy mystery series, comprising nine books, of the AVA GOLD mystery series, comprising six books; of the RACHEL GIFT mystery series, comprising ten books (and counting); of the VALERIE LAW mystery series, comprising nine books (and counting); of the PAIGE KING mystery series, comprising eight books (and counting); of the MAY MOORE mystery series, comprising eleven books; of the CORA SHIELDS mystery series, comprising eight books (and counting); of the NICKY LYONS mystery series, comprising eight books (and counting), of the CAMI LARK mystery series, comprising eight books (and counting), of the AMBER YOUNG mystery series, comprising five books (and counting), of the DAISY FORTUNE mystery series, comprising five books (and counting), of the FIONA RED mystery series, comprising five books (and counting), and of the new FAITH BOLD mystery series, comprising five books (and counting).

An avid reader and lifelong fan of the mystery and thriller genres, Blake loves to hear from you, so please feel free to visit www.blakepierceauthor.com to learn more and stay in touch.

JUST NOW (Book #7)
JUST HOPE (Book #8)

NICKY LYONS MYSTERY SERIES
ALL MINE (Book #1)
ALL HIS (Book #2)
ALL HE SEES (Book #3)
ALL ALONE (Book #4)
ALL FOR ONE (Book #5)
ALL HE TAKES (Book #6)
ALL FOR ME (Book #7)
ALL IN (Book #8)

CORA SHIELDS MYSTERY SERIES
UNDONE (Book #1)
UNWANTED (Book #2)
UNHINGED (Book #3)
UNSAID (Book #4)
UNGLUED (Book #5)
UNSTABLE (Book #6)
UNKNOWN (Book #7)
UNAWARE (Book #8)

MAY MOORE SUSPENSE THRILLER
NEVER RUN (Book #1)
NEVER TELL (Book #2)
NEVER LIVE (Book #3)
NEVER HIDE (Book #4)
NEVER FORGIVE (Book #5)
NEVER AGAIN (Book #6)
NEVER LOOK BACK (Book #7)
NEVER FORGET (Book #8)
NEVER LET GO (Book #9)
NEVER PRETEND (Book #10)
NEVER HESITATE (Book #11)

PAIGE KING MYSTERY SERIES
THE GIRL HE PINED (Book #1)
THE GIRL HE CHOSE (Book #2)
THE GIRL HE TOOK (Book #3)

THE GIRL HE WISHED (Book #4)
THE GIRL HE CROWNED (Book #5)
THE GIRL HE WATCHED (Book #6)
THE GIRL HE WANTED (Book #7)
THE GIRL HE CLAIMED (Book #8)

VALERIE LAW MYSTERY SERIES
NO MERCY (Book #1)
NO PITY (Book #2)
NO FEAR (Book #3)
NO SLEEP (Book #4)
NO QUARTER (Book #5)
NO CHANCE (Book #6)
NO REFUGE (Book #7)
NO GRACE (Book #8)
NO ESCAPE (Book #9)

RACHEL GIFT MYSTERY SERIES
HER LAST WISH (Book #1)
HER LAST CHANCE (Book #2)
HER LAST HOPE (Book #3)
HER LAST FEAR (Book #4)
HER LAST CHOICE (Book #5)
HER LAST BREATH (Book #6)
HER LAST MISTAKE (Book #7)
HER LAST DESIRE (Book #8)
HER LAST REGRET (Book #9)
HER LAST HOUR (Book #10)

AVA GOLD MYSTERY SERIES
CITY OF PREY (Book #1)
CITY OF FEAR (Book #2)
CITY OF BONES (Book #3)
CITY OF GHOSTS (Book #4)
CITY OF DEATH (Book #5)
CITY OF VICE (Book #6)

A YEAR IN EUROPE
A MURDER IN PARIS (Book #1)
DEATH IN FLORENCE (Book #2)

VENGEANCE IN VIENNA (Book #3)
A FATALITY IN SPAIN (Book #4)

ELLA DARK FBI SUSPENSE THRILLER
GIRL, ALONE (Book #1)
GIRL, TAKEN (Book #2)
GIRL, HUNTED (Book #3)
GIRL, SILENCED (Book #4)
GIRL, VANISHED (Book 5)
GIRL ERASED (Book #6)
GIRL, FORSAKEN (Book #7)
GIRL, TRAPPED (Book #8)
GIRL, EXPENDABLE (Book #9)
GIRL, ESCAPED (Book #10)
GIRL, HIS (Book #11)
GIRL, LURED (Book #12)
GIRL, MISSING (Book #13)
GIRL, UNKNOWN (Book #14)

LAURA FROST FBI SUSPENSE THRILLER
ALREADY GONE (Book #1)
ALREADY SEEN (Book #2)
ALREADY TRAPPED (Book #3)
ALREADY MISSING (Book #4)
ALREADY DEAD (Book #5)
ALREADY TAKEN (Book #6)
ALREADY CHOSEN (Book #7)
ALREADY LOST (Book #8)
ALREADY HIS (Book #9)
ALREADY LURED (Book #10)
ALREADY COLD (Book #11)

EUROPEAN VOYAGE COZY MYSTERY SERIES
MURDER (AND BAKLAVA) (Book #1)
DEATH (AND APPLE STRUDEL) (Book #2)
CRIME (AND LAGER) (Book #3)
MISFORTUNE (AND GOUDA) (Book #4)
CALAMITY (AND A DANISH) (Book #5)
MAYHEM (AND HERRING) (Book #6)

ADELE SHARP MYSTERY SERIES
LEFT TO DIE (Book #1)
LEFT TO RUN (Book #2)
LEFT TO HIDE (Book #3)
LEFT TO KILL (Book #4)
LEFT TO MURDER (Book #5)
LEFT TO ENVY (Book #6)
LEFT TO LAPSE (Book #7)
LEFT TO VANISH (Book #8)
LEFT TO HUNT (Book #9)
LEFT TO FEAR (Book #10)
LEFT TO PREY (Book #11)
LEFT TO LURE (Book #12)
LEFT TO CRAVE (Book #13)
LEFT TO LOATHE (Book #14)
LEFT TO HARM (Book #15)
LEFT TO RUIN (Book #16)

THE AU PAIR SERIES
ALMOST GONE (Book#1)
ALMOST LOST (Book #2)
ALMOST DEAD (Book #3)

ZOE PRIME MYSTERY SERIES
FACE OF DEATH (Book#1)
FACE OF MURDER (Book #2)
FACE OF FEAR (Book #3)
FACE OF MADNESS (Book #4)
FACE OF FURY (Book #5)
FACE OF DARKNESS (Book #6)

A JESSIE HUNT PSYCHOLOGICAL SUSPENSE SERIES
THE PERFECT WIFE (Book #1)
THE PERFECT BLOCK (Book #2)
THE PERFECT HOUSE (Book #3)
THE PERFECT SMILE (Book #4)
THE PERFECT LIE (Book #5)
THE PERFECT LOOK (Book #6)
THE PERFECT AFFAIR (Book #7)
THE PERFECT ALIBI (Book #8)

THE PERFECT NEIGHBOR (Book #9)
THE PERFECT DISGUISE (Book #10)
THE PERFECT SECRET (Book #11)
THE PERFECT FAÇADE (Book #12)
THE PERFECT IMPRESSION (Book #13)
THE PERFECT DECEIT (Book #14)
THE PERFECT MISTRESS (Book #15)
THE PERFECT IMAGE (Book #16)
THE PERFECT VEIL (Book #17)
THE PERFECT INDISCRETION (Book #18)
THE PERFECT RUMOR (Book #19)
THE PERFECT COUPLE (Book #20)
THE PERFECT MURDER (Book #21)
THE PERFECT HUSBAND (Book #22)
THE PERFECT SCANDAL (Book #23)
THE PERFECT MASK (Book #24)
THE PERFECT RUSE (Book #25)
THE PERFECT VENEER (Book #26)
THE PERFECT PEOPLE (Book #27)
THE PERFECT WITNESS (Book #28)

CHLOE FINE PSYCHOLOGICAL SUSPENSE SERIES
NEXT DOOR (Book #1)
A NEIGHBOR'S LIE (Book #2)
CUL DE SAC (Book #3)
SILENT NEIGHBOR (Book #4)
HOMECOMING (Book #5)
TINTED WINDOWS (Book #6)

KATE WISE MYSTERY SERIES
IF SHE KNEW (Book #1)
IF SHE SAW (Book #2)
IF SHE RAN (Book #3)
IF SHE HID (Book #4)
IF SHE FLED (Book #5)
IF SHE FEARED (Book #6)
IF SHE HEARD (Book #7)

THE MAKING OF RILEY PAIGE SERIES
WATCHING (Book #1)

WAITING (Book #2)
LURING (Book #3)
TAKING (Book #4)
STALKING (Book #5)
KILLING (Book #6)

RILEY PAIGE MYSTERY SERIES
ONCE GONE (Book #1)
ONCE TAKEN (Book #2)
ONCE CRAVED (Book #3)
ONCE LURED (Book #4)
ONCE HUNTED (Book #5)
ONCE PINED (Book #6)
ONCE FORSAKEN (Book #7)
ONCE COLD (Book #8)
ONCE STALKED (Book #9)
ONCE LOST (Book #10)
ONCE BURIED (Book #11)
ONCE BOUND (Book #12)
ONCE TRAPPED (Book #13)
ONCE DORMANT (Book #14)
ONCE SHUNNED (Book #15)
ONCE MISSED (Book #16)
ONCE CHOSEN (Book #17)

MACKENZIE WHITE MYSTERY SERIES
BEFORE HE KILLS (Book #1)
BEFORE HE SEES (Book #2)
BEFORE HE COVETS (Book #3)
BEFORE HE TAKES (Book #4)
BEFORE HE NEEDS (Book #5)
BEFORE HE FEELS (Book #6)
BEFORE HE SINS (Book #7)
BEFORE HE HUNTS (Book #8)
BEFORE HE PREYS (Book #9)
BEFORE HE LONGS (Book #10)
BEFORE HE LAPSES (Book #11)
BEFORE HE ENVIES (Book #12)
BEFORE HE STALKS (Book #13)
BEFORE HE HARMS (Book #14)

AVERY BLACK MYSTERY SERIES
CAUSE TO KILL (Book #1)
CAUSE TO RUN (Book #2)
CAUSE TO HIDE (Book #3)
CAUSE TO FEAR (Book #4)
CAUSE TO SAVE (Book #5)
CAUSE TO DREAD (Book #6)

KERI LOCKE MYSTERY SERIES
A TRACE OF DEATH (Book #1)
A TRACE OF MURDER (Book #2)
A TRACE OF VICE (Book #3)
A TRACE OF CRIME (Book #4)
A TRACE OF HOPE (Book #5)

Made in the USA
Monee, IL
29 December 2023

50757225R00094